D0004763

THE BIG BREAK

"The most amazing thing has happened to me. Natalie has invited me to appear in the next scene!"

"Really? That's great."

"I'm to be a customer. I've even been given a line."

"A speaking part! I see an Academy Award in your future."

"Very droll. My line is, 'Excuse me, can you recommend a good cigar?'"

"I'm sure your film debut will be just great. Congratulations, professor."

As Nick lifted his Scotch in salute, they heard a loud crash.

"Good lord," gasped Woolley. "What on earth was that?"

"It sounded like something falling," Nick said, lurching from the chair.

Following a rush of people in the direction of the trailers, he saw that a huge light had toppled and smashed to the ground barely two feet from Natalie Goodman.

"My god," she cried as Tony Biciano took her into his arms, "I could have been killed!"

Other Nicholas Chase Cigar Mysteries by
Harry Paul Lonsdale
from Avon Books

WHERE THERE'S SMOKE, THERE'S MURDER

ATTENTION: ORGANIZATIONS AND CORPORATIONS
Most Avon Books paperbacks are available at special quantity
discounts for bulk purchases for sales promotions, premiums, or
fund-raising. For information, please call or write:

**Special Markets Department, HarperCollins Publishers, Inc.,
10 East 53rd Street, New York, N.Y. 10022-5299.
Telephone: (212) 207-7528. Fax: (212) 207-7222.**

SMOKING
Out A
KILLER

A Nicholas Chase Cigar Mystery

HARRY PAUL LONSDALE

AVON BOOKS

An Imprint of HarperCollinsPublishers

This is a work of fiction. Names, characters, places, and incidents are the products of the author's imagination or are used fictitiously and are not to be construed as real. Any resemblance to actual events, locales, organizations, or persons, living or dead, is entirely coincidental.

AVON BOOKS
An Imprint of HarperCollins*Publishers*
10 East 53rd Street
New York, New York 10022-5299

Copyright © 2000 by H. Paul Jeffers
Inside cover author photo by Kevin Gordon
Library of Congress Catalog Card Number: 99-96771
ISBN: 0-380-80299-6
www.avonbooks.com

All rights reserved. No part of this book may be used or reproduced in any manner whatsoever without written permission, except in the case of brief quotations embodied in critical articles and reviews. For information address Avon Books, an Imprint of HarperCollins Publishers.

First Avon Books paperback printing: May 2000

Avon Trademark Reg. U.S. Pat. Off. and in Other Countries, Marca Registrada, Hecho en U.S.A.
HarperCollins ® is a trademark of HarperCollins Publishers Inc.

Printed in the U.S.A.

WCD   10 9 8 7 6 5 4 3 2 1

If you purchased this book without a cover, you should be aware that this book is stolen property. It was reported as "unsold and destroyed" to the publisher, and neither the author nor the publisher has received any payment for this "stripped book."

For Norma and the memory of Sal

Some minds are often tossed
By tempests like a tar;
I always seem in port,
So I have my cigar.

—*The Cigar,* THOMAS HOOD

PART I

Lights, Camera, Cigars

One

CONFIRMATION THAT A movie would actually be made of Roger Woolley's detective novel was contained in a memorandum:

NEW MILLENNIUM FILMS

TO: Mr. Nicholas Chase, The Happy Smoking Ground Tobacco Shop Cambridge, Massachusetts

FROM: Natalie Goodman, Chairman, CEO, Executive Producer

I am delighted that negotiations have been completed between New Millennium Films and Roger Woolley for film rights to his mystery novel *Smoking Out a Killer*. Our intention is to have a final script ready in two months and to begin preproduction work immediately. This will involve a visit to your store by a production assistant to survey the layout prior to the arrival of the crew and cast for the commencement of principal shooting, probably the week thereafter.

I am very excited about this project and I look forward to meeting the brilliant detective whose work inspired the book.

That Woolley's novel about a series of murders whose motivation was rooted in an incident during the Second World War had become a runaway best-seller had been a surprise to the publisher, but not to Woolley.

"It was the dust jacket," he explained as he chatted with Nick in Nick's apartment above The Happy Smoking Ground. He held a Partagas Corona cigar in one hand and a check for half the money Natalie Goodman was paying for the screen rights. "It's widely held that you can't judge a book by its cover. Nonsense! Put a Nazi swastika on the front, and it will *sell*. As proof I offer not only the sales of *Smoking Out a Killer,* but a novel of mine published in the 1980s about a murder in a New York City jazz club in the 1930s."

"*Death at the Double Deuces,*" said Nick. "A hell of a nice read. I liked your detective, Jake Elwell. Making him an amateur jazz saxophone player was a clever touch."

Woolley grinned. "Mr. Elwell has paid my rent for quite a few years now. But getting back to my premise that a swastika on a book jacket draws readers like flies to honey. The book, as you'll recall, involved a gang of Nazi sympathizers in America and had the Nazi insignia on the cover. Stores couldn't keep it in stock. And it's been selling continually in the French version for almost twenty years because that edition, which the Paris publisher entitled *Jazz Gang,* also bears a swastika on the cover."

Nick studied the long gray ash of his H. Upmann. "It's probably still selling so well in France because the French have always been nuts about jazz."

"By that reasoning you could contend that sales of *Smoking Out a Killer* have been good not because it's a compelling mystery yarn with a fascinating main character, based on yourself and your amazing detective work in that case, but because the timing was right in latching onto the current mania for cigar smoking."

"The reason your books do well, Professor, is the talent of the author. *Smoking Out a Killer* is a hell of a fine piece of writing. Your best yet."

"I am in total agreement!"

"Will you be writing the screenplay?"

"Heavens, no. I haven't a clue as to how to write a movie. And this dog is too old to learn new tricks. I don't have your agility in switching from one occupation to another, as you showed in going from police work to owning a tobacco shop. I've expressed my hope to Natalie Goodman that whoever she chooses to write the screenplay does justice to your character in the book. She's eager to meet you, by the way. I'm sure you'll find her fascinating. She's one of the most remarkable women I've ever known, perhaps *the* most remarkable."

Nick took a puff of his cigar and gazed fondly at the lean, elderly figure lounging on a worn yellow couch. "You surprise me, Professor."

"In what way?"

"How does a retired Harvard don happen to know a movie producer?"

"Politics brought us together in 1972," said Woolley, carefully placing the film rights check on a table. "We were both campus radicals rallying to the lost cause of George McGovern. I was an associate professor at Harvard. She was a spirited Radcliffe undergraduate." He paused to puff and stroke a gray Vandyke beard. "She was Natalie Eveland then. During a rambunctious demonstration in Harvard Square against the Vietnam War, we were arrested together. We kept in contact for a few years, but less and less frequently, and then not at all, until I received a letter a few months ago complimenting me on *Smoking Out a Killer* and inquiring about the availability of the film rights. The name Goodman meant nothing to me at the time. I've since learned that she'd married three times and was thrice widowed, the latest being an ex-Sixties radical named Goodman, who made it big in the Wall Street boom of the 1980s. When he died a few years ago, he left Natalie a fortune, which she used to form a film production company."

"From the antiwar movement to her own movie studio," said Nick. "Natalie's life could make a pretty good film itself."

"Oh, there's much more to Natalie's story. When she suddenly reappeared in my life, I did a bit of research. She's a major bankroller of politicians on the far left wing of the Democratic Party, but very quietly. Unlike Hollywood liberals such as Barbra Streisand and Steven Spielberg who were so visible in their support of President Clinton, she's always shunned the limelight. She prefers to dole out her money and either arm-twist wealthy friends into ponying up at discreet dinners in her Trump Tower suite or dragoon fat cats onto her motor yacht, *Murder Two,* and whisk them to long weekends far from the snooping lenses of the news media at her palatial summer home. It's on one of the windswept and rocky outcroppings off the coast of Maine known as the Isles of Shoals."

"Did you say *Murder Two*? What a name for a yacht."

"*Murder Two* was Natalie's first venture into movie making. Evidently, she prefers films with a lot of action and drama."

"Well, I hope the lady does justice to your novel," said Nick, raising a glass of cognac in a toast. "Here's to your work making it to the big screen."

"Thank you, but I'm less interested in how my words translate into cinema than I am in learning who will be the character of Rick Gordon, that is to say, who will be portraying you."

"Well, Bogart's dead," said Nick, turning in a battered leather chair to lift a bottle of the cognac they were drinking, "and so, alas, is Gary Cooper. I'll just have to place my trust in your friend Natalie."

"I've heard from my literary agent she's trying to sign up Harry Hardin."

Nick poured cognac into his emptied glass. "Never heard of him."

With a look of astonishment, Woolley exclaimed, "*Operation Rescue*! *Deep Space Ten*! Quite handsome. He's just completed a remake of *The Maltese Falcon,* playing Sam Spade."

Nick sipped the cognac. "Why do they insist on remaking classics? They're never as good as the originals. Bogie must be spinning in his grave, not to mention Dashiell Hammett."

"There's much of Bogart in Harry Hardin."

"I wouldn't know. The last movie I saw was that Disney cartoon *Beauty and the Beast*. I took my grandchildren. Before that I saw Woody Allen's *Manhattan Murder Mystery*. The girl who played his wife was very good. Diane something. But this Harry Hardin guy is new to me."

"With him starring, a movie is a guaranteed box office draw. His pictures have plenty of action for the younger set. Women love him, men envy him."

"If he's going to play me," Nick said, reaching out to replenish Woolley's drink, "I hope he's a cigar smoker."

"Oh he is. *Cigar Smoker* magazine put him on its cover twice."

Nick thought a moment. "Describe him to me again."

"Rugged good looks, thick brown hair, a small scar on his chin." Woolley took a sip of the cognac. "A more athletic Bogart."

Nick remembered the magazine covers. "Isn't he a bit young to be playing me, I mean Rick Gordon? It seems to me that age-wise your friend Natalie Goodman should be talking to Sean Connery. But what do I know about box office draws? I'm just an out-of-shape retired cop who runs a cigar store and happens to rent the top floor of the building to an ex-professor who's now an author of detective novels."

"A serendipitous arrangement that's served us well. Who could have imagined fifteen years ago when you came to Cambridge and bought a building from me for your cigar store that we would wind up as characters in a Harry Hardin movie?"

"If your old cell mate Natalie Goodman thinks Harry Hardin's the right guy to play Rick Gordon, who am I to argue?"

"If my memory serves, you could argue with Natalie till the cows come home and it would do you no good."

Two

"I THINK HARRY Hardin will be perfect in the part," asserted Peg Baron that night, toying with a long strand of her auburn hair as Nick sipped black coffee from a gold-toned mug with his name on it in the upstairs cigar room of Farley's restaurant. "Granted, he's younger than you, with only a few strands of gray hair instead of your silver mane, and in a lot better shape," she continued, poking a finger into Nick's soft, ample belly, "but he's definitely got that Nick Chase edge that age, too much food and drink, and way too many stogies cannot dull."

Nick set down the mug and puffed his cigar. "What the hell's that mean? What edge?"

"The thing about you that makes a woman uncertain if she's going to get kissed and, hopefully, laid, and a man wondering if he could end up getting socked in the jaw."

"You've been reading too many of Woolley's hard-boiled Jake Elwell detective novels."

Peg lifted a plain white coffee cup. "Will someone play me, or am I already on the cutting room floor?"

"I am not privy to what's in the script."

"Nicole Kidman would be good as me, don't you think?"

"I have no idea."

"If you'd forego Bruins hockey games and the Red Sox and take me to a movie once in a while, you'd know Nicole

8

Kidman. And that dreamboat hubby of hers."

"That being who?"

Peg let out a forlorn sigh. "Never mind, darling."

"Anyway, I've been notified to expect somebody from this movie outfit who's coming around one of these days to check out the store before they actually start making this movie."

Peg smiled over the rim of her cup. "Admit it, Nick. You are just a little bit excited by all this movie business."

"Excited? No. Interested, yes."

"It's just my luck," said Peg, "that these movie makers are coming to your store just at the time that I'll be on tour with the symphony. Otherwise, I might be discovered, as they used to say in Hollywood, and I'd abandon my cello to launch a career in pictures."

"Moviedom's loss is the Boston Symphony's gain."

"I intend to phone you from wherever I am every morning for a full report."

The next event in the making of the movie occurred three days later with the arrival in front of The Happy Smoking Ground of a yellow Porsche. Out of it bounded a muscular young man with shaggy blond hair and October-blue eyes. Wearing a tight white T-shirt and faded blue jeans that drew attention to his muscles, he had a Nikon camera with a long strap slung over his left shoulder and a clipboard in his left hand. Crossing the sidewalk in two strides, he passed the wooden Indian figure in front of the store, scaled two steps, and entered the store with the self-confidence Nick expected of a young man from Tinseltown.

"Good morning, sir," he said, approaching the sales counter. "Are you Mr. Nick Chase?"

Taking a half-smoked H. Upmann from his mouth, Nick said, "Yep."

"You look just like the character based on you in Mr. Woolley's book."

"I'm overweight and over sixty," said Nick. "Woolley was too kind."

The young man flashed a set of gleaming teeth. "The

novelist's prerogative." He stuck out a hand. "I'm Ivo Bogdanovich, no relation to the director Peter Bogdanovich,
although I wish I were. I hope you were notified that I'd
be coming here today."

"I got a memo from an associate producer, name of Tony
Biciano. It said you're going to look the place over."

"That's it. My job is to give the director, Al Leibholz,
and the cinematographer, Bernard Wolf, an idea of the layout of your store. Today I'll make a few notes and drawings
and shoot some still pictures so they'll have an idea of the
set. The production schedule calls for us to be here next
Sunday. We picked Sunday so as to not interfere too much
with the other stores on Brattle Street. All your neighbors
have been apprised by letter. And, of course, we don't want
to close down your business any more than is absolutely
necessary. We'll be shooting exteriors mostly, but the script
calls for a few scenes inside the store. I'll try to keep out
of the way of you and your customers while I'm here today."

"Monday mornings are always slow, so that's not a problem. Feel free to help yourself to some cigars."

"Thanks very much," said the young man as he began
work, "but I don't smoke."

"Ah, well," said Nick, shrugging broad shoulders, "to
each his own, Mr. Bogdanovich."

"Ivo, please. Since a major plot line of *Smoking Out a
Killer* is cigars, I guess I'll just have to get used to them,
right? So don't feel you have to put yours out because of
me."

"I won't."

On Thursday, notices from the Cambridge Police Department appeared on lampposts on both sides of Brattle
Street advising that parking would not be permitted for
twenty-four hours beginning at midnight Saturday. At six
o'clock Sunday morning various vans, automobiles, large
trucks filled with movie-making equipment, a small truck
that served as a cafeteria for cast and crew, and trailers for
use by the actors as dressing rooms arrived.

Standing beside Nick at the store's counter at seven o'clock, Roger Woolley gazed with amazement at dozens of men and women scurrying about, working to convert Brattle Street into a movie set. By eight o'clock the block had been transformed into a bizarre forest of spindly-looking poles supporting huge lights pointed at the store, interspersed with broad silver umbrellalike reflectors. In the middle of the street stood the camera and a small group of earnest-looking young men.

"My lord, Nick," Woolley muttered, "What have we wrought?"

Nick grunted. "We? You're the guy who wrote the book."

As he spoke, the man who would portray him in the movie stepped from a trailer. Much shorter and a good deal more slender than the character he was to portray, he strode toward the store. "It is truly amazing to me as a professor of history," said Woolley as they watched Hardin approach, "that America is admired around the world not for having demonstrated that free people can govern themselves and that capitalism works, but for *movies*. More people around the globe know who Harry Hardin is than can name the president of the United States."

As Woolley finished, the door opened and the actor entered. "What the President needs," he said with a laugh, "is better distribution." With an unlighted cigar in his left hand, he extended the right toward Nick. "Hello, Mr. Chase. It's a privilege to meet you."

"Call me Nick, please."

"Any tips you have as to how I should play you will be welcome."

"The band on your cigar."

Hardin held up the cigar and looked at it quizzically. "The band?"

"I always remove it. Smoking a cigar with the band is like making love to a woman with her clothes on."

"May I pass that line along to our writer?"

"If he thinks it's worth using, he's welcome to it."

"She! The writer of the hour is Sheila Stevens."

"Excuse me," interjected Woolley. "Why do you call her the writer of the hour?"

"Sheila is the third that Natalie's brought in on the project in the past six months and the fifth since Natalie acquired the rights to your book. The current script is Sheila's second try. I'm sure if we weren't locked into a production schedule, poor Sheila would be on her way out."

"It sounds like a complicated story," said Woolley.

"Between you, me, Nick, and the wooden Indian outside," said Hardin *sotto voce,* "the only thing complicating this production is the bitch in charge."

Woolley bristled. "Are you referring to Natalie Goodman?"

"Careful, Harry," said Nick with a frown. "Natalie Goodman and Roger Woolley are not just business associates. They're old jail mates."

The door opened, and Ivo Bogdanovich announced, "We're ready for you, Harry."

Hardin made a little bow. "Excuse me, fellas, it's star time."

Looking through the window, Nick and Woolley watched as Hardin stood in front of the store and gazed upward. "This must be the scene," whispered Woolley, "where you, that is Rick, look up and see the light on in my, that is Professor Lamb's, apartment window, thereby eliminating him as a murder suspect." With a nudge to Nick's ribs he added, "If you look behind the camera, you'll see Natalie Goodman."

A tall, attractive, dark-haired woman of middle age in a smart navy-blue blouse and gray slacks, she suddenly threw up her arms and appeared to be shouting at a man standing to the left of the camera. A moment later, the scene was shot again. Evidently satisfied with the second take, she barged past Hardin without a word and toward the store.

"A very simple scene, and that disaster of a director couldn't get it on the first take," she said, bursting in. "At the rate Al Leibholz is moving, we'll be in Cambridge the entire damned week. I ought to can his ass."

"Still the firebrand I knew way back when," exclaimed

Woolley, advancing toward her with open arms.

She kissed his cheek. "Professor, you haven't changed a whit. Still *the* fixed point in a universe constantly changing for the worse." She held out a hand to Nick. "Hardly a propitious way for us to meet at last, but that's the movie business." She scowled through the window. "If I had the time and the budget, I'd fire cast and crew and start over." Turning to Nick, she patted his cheek. "You must be thinking that I am indeed the bitch everyone says I am. Don't try to deny that's what you've been told."

"I never base an opinion about someone on what I've been told," Nick said. "I decide on my own if someone's a bitch."

"Good. You'll have that opportunity over dinner this evening at Farley's. That is your favorite restaurant, I believe?"

"Since the day the place opened! How did you know?"

"I made it my business to learn more about you as a detective than I read in Professor Woolley's book," she said, walking toward the door. "We are booked for eight o'clock in the upstairs cigar room." She smiled affectionately at Woolley. "Tonight must be only Nick and me, ex-cop and ex-revolutionary. You and I will have our own special evening recalling days of auld lang syne when we were a couple of antiestablishment ball busters. Okay, my darling?"

As she left the store, Woolley muttered. "She is still a most remarkable woman."

"Astonishing, actually," Nick said through a cloud of cigar smoke. "It will be interesting to see what's worrying her."

Woolley gave Nick's back a slap. "That's what I like about you, Nick. You immediately turn something as simple as a social invitation into a mystery."

"When a woman like that asks an ex-cop to dinner," Nick said as he watched her gesticulating forcefully while she again berated the director, "she's either in trouble or expects to be."

Three

AROUND NOON NICK stood across Brattle Street from The Happy Smoking Ground to watch the filming of a scene in front of the store between Harry Hardin and Felix Marlowe. A courtly-looking, elderly actor who'd been a star in the 1950s, he was making a comeback in the role of the Professor Woolley character. But he and Hardin had barely begun when Natalie Goodman shouted from behind the camera, "No, no. Cut! This will never do. Felix, you're playing it way over the top. Good lord, man, we're in a new century!"

This outburst was followed by a lengthy argument with associate producer Rich Edwards, at the end of which he threw up his arms. "All right, all right, we'll shoot it again after lunch."

Sidling next to Nick, Harry Hardin whispered, "See what I mean? What a bitch. Did you see her jump all over Felix? Uncalled for! Did you find anything wrong with that take?"

"It seemed fine to me, but my experience with making movies is limited to one day back in 1956. I was a patrolman with the NYPD assigned to keep traffic and spectators off the block of West Fifty-second Street between Fifth and Sixth Avenues. They were filming inside the '21' club, making the Burt Lancaster-Tony Curtis film, *Sweet Smell of Success.*"

"Before my time, but a truly great film. If it's ever re-made, I'd love to sink my teeth into the Burt Lancaster role. J. J. Hunsecker! What a rat. I'd give my right nut to play a rat. Better yet, I'd like to play a murderer. But only if my victim is someone like Natalie. That way I'd have the sympathy of the audience. It's as if she goes out of her way to piss people off. If it weren't for her constant inter-ruptions, we'd have shot four scenes by now. Instead, we've done two."

"Hopefully, things will go faster after lunch."

"Only if she chokes to death on a sandwich. Would you care to join me for lunch in my trailer, Nick?"

"Thanks, but I've promised Woolley I'd lunch with him and Felix Marlowe in Woolley's apartment."

"You'll enjoy Felix," said Hardin. "He's a gentleman of the old school and a film icon who deserves better treatment than he's getting on this picture."

When Nick entered Woolley's apartment a few minutes later, the living room was already pungent with smoke from two briar pipes as Woolley and Marlowe stood by a tow-ering bookcase with two shelves of Woolley's detective novels. Tall, spare, wearing a brown tweed jacket with suede elbow patches, and with a glued-on gray-streaked Vandyke beard, the elderly actor appeared to be Woolley's twin.

"Ah, here's the man himself," declared Woolley, turning toward the door. "Nick, I was just telling Felix your life story."

"And quite a tale it is," said Marlowe.

The deep baritone voice carried Nick back in time to Saturday movie matinees when the actor was the Napoleon of evil, Professor Moriarty, engaged in a battle of wits with the peerless Basil Rathbone as Sherlock Holmes. And to an afternoon in Miss Kelly's English class when she showed a film with Felix Marlowe as *Hamlet*.

"What a delight to meet you, Mr. Marlowe," said Nick. "Welcome to Cambridge."

"It's a return to my youth, actually. I spent two years

strutting the stage with the Hasty Pudding Club at Harvard before dropping out to try my wings on Broadway, then Hollywood."

"And we are all the better for it."

"Most kind of you, sir."

"While you two engage in mutual admiration," declared Woolley, "I'll see about getting us lunch. Won't be a minute. Sit! Sit!"

"You've returned to the screen in a very challenging role," said Nick, plopping into an armchair and taking a cigar from a pocket case, "but I can't imagine anyone capturing Woolley's irascible nature better than you. Natalie Goodman's casting of you in the part was a stroke of sheer genius."

"If my performance a few minutes ago is any measure," Marlowe said, sitting on a couch next to the table where Woolley wrote his novels on an old Underwood upright typewriter, "the lady may be regretting that choice."

"For what it's worth, I think that scene went very well. So did Harry Hardin."

Woolley reappeared carrying a tray of sandwiches. "I thought the way Natalie treated you was outrageous."

"You don't know what outrageous is," said Marlowe, "unless you've been directed by an Otto Preminger or a John Ford. Compared to those tyrants, Natalie Goodman is an angel. Were I to have coaxed several millions of dollars from some very scary people to make a film and an old fart such as myself ruined a scene, I'd be pretty impatient."

Woolley sat beside the actor. "Impatient? Natalie was downright rude, and not just to you. She's done nothing but castigate the director—what's his name?"

"Al Leibholz. She's been nagging him from the start. I wouldn't be at all surprised if he were replaced. But that's not unusual, especially when a film is in its early stages of production. *Gone With the Wind* had at least four directors, if I recall properly. The making of motion pictures has always been a balancing of personalities. I can name three directors and half-a-dozen producers in my day whom I could have murdered and been found not guilty on the grounds of justifiable homicide, assuming the jury consisted of actors and directors. I expect Natalie will find things going much more smoothly this afternoon."

Promptly at one o'clock, she appeared in the company of a handsome young man wearing black sunglasses, a blue denim shirt opened halfway to the waist to reveal a chiseled chest, tight black jeans, and tan boots. Coming up to Nick, she introduced him as Tony Biciano.

As they shook hands, Nick said, "It's nice to be able to put a face on the name I read at the bottom of so many letters and memos."

"I hope everything I said in them is working out as you expected. I'm afraid no amount of letters and memos can ever prepare someone for the shock of a motion picture crew showing up on the doorstep. But I assure you, Nick, we'll be out of your hair sometime tonight and you can get back to normalcy."

"That's enough small talk, Tony," Natalie snapped. "Go and round up everyone we need to shoot this scene that should have been wrapped hours ago. I've invited Nick to dinner at eight, I leave for the island in the morning, and I do not intend to allow a bunch of incompetents to upset my schedule."

Four

"PROFESSOR, THERE'S BEEN a tragic death."

"Not in your delightful family, I hope, Rick."

"Thank God, no."

"Then it has to be another in the rapidly dwindling phalanx of which I spoke yesterday. Which of my colleagues has at last journeyed into what Shakespeare termed that undiscovered country from whose bourn no traveler returns?"

Watching the scene, Nick sat in a folding chair with a blue canvas seat and backrest. Set up for him by Ivo Bogdanovich on a spot across Brattle Street, it allowed him to see between supports of what seemed to be a canopy of metallic umbrellas whose purpose was to reflect light on Felix Marlowe and Harry Hardin. They stood next to the wooden Indian, although in Woolley's book and in reality they'd spoken in Woolley's apartment.

"It was Jerome Stanley."

"A heart attack?"

"He was murdered."

"Cut! It's a keeper," announced Al Leibholz. Tall and burly, with a New York Yankees baseball cap slanted so low it almost covered his broad face, he glanced at a clipboard. "I want us set up inside and ready to go in twenty minutes."

As people who for a few moments had stood as still and silent as figures in a painting sprang to life, Bogdanovich appeared at Nick's side. "I'm gonna have to move you and your chair, Nick. The grips have to strike these reflectors."

"Grips," said Nick, chuckling as he surrendered the chair. "You movie people certainly have a colorful jargon."

"Doesn't every profession? I'm sure you used plenty of colorful phrases and words when you were a police officer. And there must be special words in the cigar store business."

"True, most of them Spanish."

"If you'd like a drink, there's a bar by the catering wagon."

"A drink sounds great. Will you have one with me?"

"It's tempting, but if the boss were to find me having a drink . . . It wouldn't be a pretty sight."

Nick looked round. "If the boss you refer to is Natalie Goodman, she seems to have disappeared."

"She's in her trailer having a . . . conference . . . with Tony Biciano," said Bogdanovich with a sly smile, "known by everyone on this production as her best boy."

"Do I detect an inside joke? Am I correct in deducing that there's something going on beside movie making between Natalie and Tony?"

The smile stretched to a grin. "You are a good detective. Now, if you'll excuse me—"

"May I detain you long enough for you to answer a question about the scene I just saw?"

"Of course."

"What's the reasoning in moving it from Woolley's apartment?"

"Professor Woolley's apartment just wasn't right. We're having a much better one built on a sound stage."

"Why not make the entire film on a sound stage?"

"That was the intention, but Natalie decided to take a trip down memory lane by shooting part of the picture here in Cambridge. And she's got a fabulous summer home on an island off the coast of Maine that she's going to tomorrow."

"Are you telling me that Natalie decided to go on location just to get a dose of nostalgia and because Cambridge is close to her summer place?"

Boganovich grinned. "Everything she does goes straight into the budget."

"You don't care much for her, do you?"

"There you go, detecting again."

"Why don't you like her?"

"Are you trying to get me in trouble?"

"I'm an old detective. I'm naturally curious."

Bogdanovich looked furtively toward Natalie's trailer. "I can tell you a joke."

"I'm a guy who enjoys a laugh."

"Natalie asks her lawyer, another piece of work named Simon Cane, 'Simon, why does everyone take an instant dislike to me?' Simon replies, 'It saves time.' Now I really must get to work. Enjoy your drink."

Finding himself alone at the catering trailer, Nick studied an astonishing array of liquor set up on a folding table with a white paper cloth. He chose a tall, green, triangular bottle of Glenfiddich single malt scotch. He half filled a clear plastic cup that approximated an old fashioned glass, sat on another folding chair with a blue canvas seat, and placed the drink on the right arm of the chair. He fished one of three H. Upmann cigars from his shirt pocket, dug out a clipper and a box of long wooden matches from the same pocket, and performed the ritual of cutting and lighting. Settled back in the chair, he alternately sipped and smoked surrounded by the activities of movie making that suddenly seemed very much like a crime scene.

Each required an assortment of professionals with special skills who worked alone yet realized they were members of a team. Pondering this, he thought about all he'd seen during the day of shooting and decided that the analogy held. What was a film but an amalgam of individual parts, snippets of scenes that appeared to have nothing to do with one another, until an editor put them together in a way that made sense? At a crime scene the bits were fingerprints, impressions left by shoes, strands of hair, thread, fibers, and other detritus that ultimately had to be pieced together to prove how a crime had been committed, why, and if all went well, by whom.

The only difference between a movie and a criminal case, he thought, as he savored the complementary flavors of malt scotch and tobacco, was that one was shown on a screen and the other was presented to a jury. The success of one was found in reviews of film critics, who, like the emperors of Rome presiding over gladiatorial contests, rendered judgment with a thumb up or down, and by millions of people who plunked down money at box offices all over the country and around the world and in rentals at video stores. Judgment of a criminal case was rendered by twelve people in a verdict.

What was a good movie or a successful criminal case, after all was said and done, but a combination of small parts—scenes or evidence—skillfully woven from beginning to end where all the elements of plot, character, setting, and atmosphere were knitted into a compelling story?

"Nick, dear boy," said Roger Woolley so joltingly that Nick nearly spilled the scotch, "you look positively lost in reverie. Not having second thoughts, I hope?"

"Second thoughts? About what?"

"About having agreed to this invasion of your emporium by movie makers."

Nick puffed the cigar. "Not at all. I'm enjoying it. And you?"

"The most amazing thing has happened to me. Natalie has invited me to appear in the next scene!"

"Really? That's great."

"I'm to be a customer. I've even been given a line."

"A speaking part! I see an Academy Award in your future."

"Very droll. My line is, 'Excuse me, can you recommend a good cigar?' "

"That's casting against character. You're usually a pipe smoker."

With a look of exasperation, Woolley exclaimed, "I don't actually *smoke* the cigar."

"I'm sure your film debut will be just great. Congratulations, Professor."

As Nick lifted his scotch in salute, they heard a loud crash.

"Good lord," gasped Woolley. "What on earth was that?"

"It sounded like something falling," Nick said, lurching from the chair.

Following a rush of people in the direction of the trailers, he saw that a huge light had toppled and smashed to the ground barely two feet from Natalie Goodman.

"My god," she cried as Tony Biciano took her into his arms, "I could have been killed!"

PART II

Cut to the Chase

Five

THE BRASS SIGN marking Farley's restaurant read SERVING
DISTINCTIVE IRISH FOOD AND DRINKS SINCE 1933. This was
true, but not at its present location. Between the start of
Prohibition in 1920 and Repeal in 1933 it had been a waterfront speakeasy on Commercial Street in Boston, then a
popular North End restaurant. Forced into relocating to
clear the way for two supporting columns of the express-
way subsequently named in honor of John "Honey Fitz"
Fitzgerald, grandfather of the late President John F. Kennedy, the owner, Peter John (P.J.) Farley, chose to leave
Boston for a location he believed safe from urban renewal.
He opened the doors of a new restaurant on Waterhouse
Street, Cambridge, an easy walk for thirsty Harvard stu-
dents and dons, including Professor Roger Woolley. Four
years after Woolley introduced Nick Chase to the place, a
large second-floor room that had been reserved for private
parties and banquets was converted to the cigar room,
where Nick now nursed a drink and waited for Natalie.

    She arrived in the smoky, wood-paneled, and a little too
dark room at ten past eight. Escorted to Nick's table by a
genuine Irish waitress named Maggie Tinney, she carried a
small silver-toned purse and wore a black cocktail dress
with a rope of pearls. A flowery silk scarf draped her left
shoulder.

"I'm sorry for being late, Nick," she said, sitting. "My limo driver took the wrong way, and we were stuck in traffic. I should have stayed at a hotel here in Cambridge, but I've got a sentimental spot in my heart for the Copley Plaza. I was arrested in its lobby during a protest in 1972 against a speech being made there by President Nixon."

Maggie asked, "May I get you a drink?"

"What's that you're having, Nick?"

"Jameson's Irish whiskey."

"Very appropriate to the place. I'll have the same."

As the waitress withdrew, Nick said, "You appear to have recovered nicely from your encounter with a falling light."

"Thank god Tony was there to pull me aside."

"Well, I'm glad to see that you're none the worse for it."

"As I'm sure you've noticed, Nick," she said, opening the purse and taking out a pack of cigarettes, "I'm not one for shilly-shallying."

Nick picked up a box of wooden matches, struck one, and held it as she lit her cigarette. "Your forthrightness has come to my attention."

"Having read Professor Woolley's book several times, I believe I know very well how your mind works. Therefore, I presume you immediately surmised when I asked you to dinner that I had an ulterior motive."

"Ulterior motive! Sounds like a movie title."

"Am I correct in my assumption?"

"Yes."

"Good, then I'll cut to the chase. Pardon the pun on your name!"

"I'm used to it."

Maggie returned with the whiskey.

"I invited you to dinner," Natalie continued as Maggie departed, "because I am in very grave danger."

"What sort of danger?"

"Murder. You witnessed the latest attempt this afternoon."

"The accident of the light?"

"Trust me, Nick, it was not an accident. Doesn't it strike

you as curious that it toppled just as I stepped from my trailer?"

"Yet it missed hitting you."

She all but gulped the whiskey. "Not by much."

"You said you believe this was the latest attempt on your life?"

"There have been at least two others."

"When and where?"

"They occurred soon after we began preproduction meetings on *Smoking Out a Killer* at my ranch above Santa Barbara."

"Do you believe there's a significance in the timing?"

"Possibly."

"Why?"

"It's just a feeling that came over me."

"What else was happening in your life at that time?"

"Everything was going swimmingly with the business."

"How about personally?"

"By personally, shall I assume you mean my love life?"

"You can't get any more personal than that. Had someone new come into your life that somebody might not have been happy about?"

"Obviously, you've picked up gossip about me and Tony Biciano."

"When did your relationship with him begin?"

"It was established before I began negotiations to buy Woolley's book. I've heard the joke about Tony being my best boy. But he means more to me than a convenient roll in the hay. We are lovers in the true meaning of the word. I love him and he loves me. When this picture is finished, I intend to marry him, no matter what anyone says or thinks."

Nick lifted his glass in a toast. "Good for you."

"Yes, he is good for me."

"I didn't mean—"

"I know what you meant," she said as Nick finished his drink "And I also know that some people in the business see Tony as an opportunist who hopes to use me to get ahead in the film industry. And candidly, I know a few people who shudder at the possibility that I will gradually turn over the running of the company to him."

"Such as who?"

"Associates in my production company. Money people."

"I was under the impression that you owned New Millennium Films."

"I own fifty-one percent. The remaining portion is divided between four investors. But as we undertake projects, we seek outside financing. I'm not as fortunate as George Lucas, who has a personal fortune with which to finance his films."

"Are any of your partners unhappy with the way you run the business?"

"Three are old friends of my late husband, who have never questioned the way I control the company. The fourth, Rich Edwards, has been in the film industry for many years and is a wizard at getting financing. He was so enthusiastic about the current project that he lined up most of the money with a couple of phone calls. Rich will be listed in the credits as coproducer and on the next production he'll be the producer. I think so highly of him that I've got my attorney, Simon Cane, drawing up papers to guarantee Rich a role in New Millennium when I step down."

"You're planning on stepping down?"

"I'll be fifty next year. I've been working all my life. It's time to start thinking ahead to a day when I should, as the saying goes, stop and smell the roses. God and the box office receipts from *Smoking Out a Killer* permitting, I intend to start doing so by marrying Tony. Assuming I'm not murdered first."

"Before I turned to peddling tobacco as a way of smelling the roses, it was my experience in thirty or so years as a homicide cop that there are four motives for murder: love and the other side of that coin, hate; revenge; and greed."

"I can nominate several people as contenders in those categories. That's why I invited you to dinner. I want you to investigate."

"For me to do that, Natalie, I'd have to dig into your entire life. I've got a business of my own to run. What you need, if you're serious about this, is a professional private detective. I'll be delighted to give you the names of four of the best, two in New York, an excellent young man in Los Angeles, and one in Honolulu."

"How long would it be before the tabloids and TV shows like *Show Business Today* and *Extra* ran a story about some gumshoe being hired by Natalie Goodman to check up on her friends and associates? I need you to do this for me, Nick."

"First of all, I'm not in the detective game anymore. Secondly, I can't abandon The Happy Smoking Ground to go snooping around Hollywood because you have this vague feeling that someone is out to murder you."

"But someone is."

"There's no evidence of that."

"The incident this afternoon."

"The falling over of that light looked like an accident to me, Natalie."

"You're a man with a logical mind. Apply it now, please, to the fact that I invited you to dine with me this evening to tell you of my fear that someone is out to kill me *before* that light nearly did the job. What happened today wasn't the first such incident. When I was coming back from Santa Barbara after the preproduction meetings, someone in a blue van tried to run me off the freeway."

"Did you report it to the police?"

"No."

"Why not, if you thought that someone wished you dead?"

"At the time I attributed the incident to the usual crazy driving on the freeway. I didn't see it for what it was until a few days later at my house in the mountains above Santa Barbara."

"What happened then?"

"I found a bullet hole in a living room window."

"Did you report it to the police?"

"A sheriff's deputy who investigated attributed it to a hunter's stray shot."

"Each of these incidents can be explained as chance events. Coincidence!"

"In Professor Woolley's book he wrote that you don't believe in coincidences."

"Even if I were to concede that each of these three events might have been an attempt on your life, what can I possibly do about it? I'm not in a position to launch an investigation of all the people in your life, past and present, which is what I'd have to do. It's entirely possible that someone you knew years ago when you were a radical activist could have decided to settle up on a long-simmering score."

"The falling light proves that whoever wants to kill me was on the set today."

"Or had an accomplice."

Natalie gasped, "Oh, Nick, that possibility never occurred to me."

Maggie appeared again. "Are you ready to order?"

Natalie touched Nick's hand lightly. "You choose, dear."

"I usually have the broiled lamb chops and baked potato."

"The same for me, miss."

"How do you prefer them cooked, ma'am?"

"Medium to well done And I'd better have another whiskey."

"Yes, ma'am."

As Maggie departed, Nick saw that Natalie's hands were shaking.

"Nick, I am terrified. I'm begging you to help me."

"You haven't given me a lot to go on. And excuse me for being blunt, but from what I saw and heard on the set today, there are plenty of people working for you on this movie who don't think much of you as a person."

"I know I'm not popular. It goes with the job. But how many of them could have been on the freeway or fired that shot at my house in Santa Barbara? Whoever is doing this is close to me, Nick. Very close."

"What can I do? You've wrapped up shooting in Cambridge."

"Yes. Production resumes next week on the coast."

"Then I propose that you contact one of the firms in L.A. that provide personal security to people in the movie business. Get yourself round-the-clock protection."

"Bodyguards?"

"I see no alternative."

"I do. That's why I asked you to dinner. I have a plan." Again Maggie appeared, bringing the whiskey. When she was gone, Natalie continued, "I want you to join me and a few guests for the weekend at my house on a small island near Portsmouth, New Hampshire." She opened her purse and withdrew a small piece of paper. "This is the list of guests. With the exception of Tony Biciano and Professor Woolley, you may regard them as suspects. All you have to do—"

"Is find out which one is trying to kill you."

Natalie sipped whiskey and smiled. "Exactly."

Nick took the list. "I know about Rich Edwards and that Simon Cane is your lawyer. Who are the others?"

"Nigel Wilson is a major investor in the film, who aspires to use the experience to become a movie mogul."

"Why is he on your list of potential suspects?"

"How shall I put it nicely? I suppose the polite phrase is 'spurned lover.' You see, before Tony there was Nigel."

"Yet you've remained friends?"

"We've remained business associates."

"Tell me about Clifford Branson."

"Cliffie was the original writer on *Smoking Out a Killer*."

"Why did you replace him?"

"It was a lousy script. He was not happy about being fired."

"So unhappy that you think he'd try to kill you?"

"Cliffie has two problems, alcohol and a violent nature, which drinking brings out, especially when he's feeling rejected."

"If you fired him and he resented it, why is he on your weekend guest list?"

"Should he be the one who's been trying to kill me and I didn't invite him, how could you possibly determine that it's him? Cliffie is also a delightful raconteur at parties."

Nick looked at the list. "Sheila Stevens is the current screenwriter?"

"Yes. Who told you that?"

"I don't recall. It may have been Harry Hardin."

"Did he also tell you that he and Sheila have become an item and that I don't approve?"

"Why is their relationship any of your business?"

"Everything affecting a Natalie Goodman production is my business."

"If you disapprove of them having an affair, why invite both for the weekend?"

"Again, the purpose of this weekend is to make it easier for you to investigate."

"Natalie, do you really expect one of these people to try to kill you knowing there's an ex-homicide detective on the premises?"

"Your presence on the set did not stand in the way of today's attempt. But you have made a good point. That's why I've given all the guests a perfectly plausible explanation for your joining us for the weekend. I've told them there will be entertainment. That's you. I want you to give a lecture on cigars! So, you see, you won't be viewed by the suspects as Nick Chase, detective, but as a cigar aficionado, proprietor of The Happy Smoking Ground, and the film's technical adviser. Now let's set aside the subject of my murder and enjoy our dinner, shall we?"

"There's one other name on your list. Parker Slade."

"Parker is a new, not untalented young actor with a small role in *Smoking Out a Killer*. He's Rich Edwards's latest discovery, to use a euphemism for lover. That makes the young man, if not a true suspect himself, a possible accomplice. That's for you to determine."

"Your confidence in me is flattering, but my advice is still that you abandon this charade, go back to the Coast, and get yourself some security."

"I leave for the island tomorrow with Tony. The guests will be picked up Friday morning at ten by my yacht at Rowes Wharf in Boston. It will arrive at the island in time for dinner. If you're not on board, I'm certain that one day soon you will hear that I've been murdered and you will have to live knowing you might have prevented it."

"Natalie, this is nothing less than extortion."

"Yes, it is. Blackmailing people is one of my most useful talents."

Six

TURNING ONTO BRATTLE Street just before ten o'clock, Nick found no sign of the carnival atmosphere of the day. Trucks, vans, trailers, lights, reflectors, director, crew and cast of *Smoking Out a Killer,* and the crowds of curious onlookers were gone without a trace. The woman who'd caused them to descend upon The Happy Smoking Ground was on her way back to the Copley Plaza Hotel in Boston, having survived an attempt to kill her on a Los Angeles freeway, a bullet fired through a window of her house in Santa Barbara, a crashing light, and just a few minutes ago a sniper's shot in front of Farley's.

Approaching The Happy Smoking Ground, he fixed his gaze on the wooden Indian and wished that somehow the antique symbol of the tobacconist could come to life and tell what its eyes had beheld in the moments before the light had toppled. Giving the Indian a gentle tap, he looked up to find the windows of Woolley's apartment dark. Opening a side door, he climbed stairs to his own apartment directly above the store, described by Woolley in the novel which had brought movie makers to Brattle Street as a mixture of furnishings, useful and decorative accessories, and a large array of police-related objects and souvenirs of the resident's former career as a New York City homicide detective.

In all those years, Nick thought, as he entered the living room and turned on a light, he'd never been called upon to *prevent* a murder. Taking off his jacket, he looked at a collection of images of Sherlock Holmes in porcelain and pewter. "What would you make of this fancy little mystery, Sherlock?" he asked. "Is it a one-, two-, or three-pipe problem?" Or might the sleuth of Baker Street deduce the answer while smoking a cigar from the bundle he kept in a coal scuttle?

Taking an H. Upmann from a tabletop humidor, he settled into the corner of a battered couch and drew from his shirt pocket Natalie Goodman's list of names. A moment later the door opened and Woolley barged in.

"I've spent a delightful evening with Felix Marlowe," he exclaimed. "I invoked my privileges as an ex-Harvard don to treat him to dinner at the faculty club, then conducted a tour of all the important scenes in the case which became the basis for *Smoking Out a Killer.*"

Clipping the cigar, Nick said, "Marlowe survived both ordeals, I trust?"

"What a delightful fellow Felix is. He's a veritable living history of motion pictures," said Woolley, plopping into an overstuffed chair. "How was dinner with Natalie?"

"Interesting."

"Have you accepted her invitation for this weekend?"

Nick jerked the cigar from his mouth. "How do you know about that?"

"I'm also invited."

"I know that," Nick said, lighting the cigar with a long wooden match. "But how did you know I was going to be?"

"Natalie inquired of me about asking you."

"And you said I'd accept?"

"*Au contraire, mon ami!* I told her it was most unlikely."

"Did she tell you she believes someone's trying to kill her?"

Woolley bolted upright. "She did not."

"Your old friend told me about three attempts—a van tried to run her car off a freeway, someone fired a bullet

into the window of her mountain retreat, the event this afternoon."

"What event?"

"The light that fell. And not more than half an hour ago
someone took another shot at her as we were leaving Farley's."

Woolley sat up. "My lord, was she hurt?"

"The shot missed her, but not by much."

"This is outrageous!"

"On this list," said Nick, handing it to Woolley, "are the
people she suspects. She's invited them to spend the weekend on her island and expects me to finger the would-be
killer. She said that if I didn't, her blood would be on my
hands."

"I told you she is an extraordinary woman. The forthcoming weekend has suddenly taken on a whole new dimension. Nick Chase on the case! What a thrill!"

"Because of this movie, The Happy Smoking Ground has
already lost a day's business. Now I'm going to have to
bring in Craig Spencer to run the store while I'm spending
a weekend on a godforsaken island."

"I must say, her choice of locale for you to unmask the
culprit is superb. I have for some time been mulling over
an idea for a Jake Elwell novel set in just such a spot.
However, I would face the daunting certainty of finding
myself compared to Agatha Christie's *Ten Little Indians*.
That's the trouble with Agatha. She grabbed all the good
plots and best locations."

"Do you recognize any of the names on the list?"

Woolley studied them. "I'm sorry, they're just names to
me. No, wait. I recall reading about this one in the business
section of the *Globe,* Richard Edwards. Some kind of scan-
dal."

"He's a minority shareholder in New Millennium Films
who arranged the financing for *Smoking Out a Killer*. He's
also Natalie's designated heir to run the company when she
decides to chuck the movie business and pursue paradise
with Tony Biciano."

Woolley scowled. "Why, he's barely half her age."

"Would you be so shocked if their ages were reversed?"

"I certainly would."

"The Simon Cane on the list is Natalie's lawyer."

"She suspects her attorney of possibly wanting to kill her? It's usually the other way round, a client wanting to kill the lawyer."

"I'm glad you'll be around this weekend. I'll require your help."

Woolley beamed. "In what way?"

"You're a mystery novelist. You have brilliant insights into character."

"This is true only of the people I invent for my books."

"I didn't find much invention in *Smoking Out a Killer*. Your ex-detective, Rick Gordon, owns a tobacco shop in Cambridge. He's got a son who's a crime reporter for a newspaper in Boston. The son's wife is a Boston Police Department criminologist. They have two charming kids, a boy and a girl. Rick's lady friend plays cello for the BSO. All you did was change names. And your portrait of me could have sufficed for a description on a wanted poster. Did you have to point out that in my years as a cop I'd gained twenty pounds, that my waistline had gone from thirty-eight to forty-two, and that my brown hair had gotten thinner and gone to gray?"

"But I did note that you are as sharp today as you've ever been. Natalie Goodman evidently is convinced of it. She's entrusted her life to you."

"Nonsense. She's in as much danger as you are."

"Then why have you agreed to spend a weekend at her island retreat?"

"Because I'm a sap."

Woolley shook his head slowly. "You are going because deep inside your brain a little voice is saying, 'Perhaps someone *is* intent on murdering this woman.' That little voice is your conscience. If there is any truth about you in *Smoking Out a Killer*, Nick, it's that you are not a man who'd turn his back on someone crying out to you in distress, real or imagined. Frankly, I don't believe it's far-fetched that someone might be trying to murder Natalie

Goodman. It will be interesting to watch you in action
again."

Nick cracked a smile. "I see what you're up to."

"Whatever do you mean?"

"You're already working on turning this wild goose
chase into a second Rick Gordon detective novel and hoping it will lead to another lucrative movie deal. If I'm to
be the pattern for Rick I ought to get a cut of your take."

"That's fine with me,"said Woolley, fishing a bent black
briar pipe from one coat pocket and a tobacco pouch from
the other. "However, if you are truly interested in cashing
in on your adventures in homicide, you should write your
memoirs. I'd be delighted to put you in touch with my
literary agent."

"Me write another of those my-life-as-a-cop books? No,
thanks."

Silence descended as Woolley carefully packed his pipe
and lit it with one of Nick's matches. Waving a hand to
disperse a cloud of pungent smoke engulfing his head, he
settled back in the chair contentedly and recited:

> *"And so, as we sat, we reasoned still*
> *Of fate and fortune, of human will,*
> *And what are the purposes men fulfill."*

Nick puffed his cigar. "You're in a mellow mood."

"And why shouldn't I be? I've passed a day seeing my
work translated into a movie, had a very good dinner, an
evening of stimulating conversation with a gentleman of
my generation, and now I'm here in very pleasant surround-
ings, smoking with a brilliant detective, who is about to
undertake the most challenging case of his career. It's a
moment such as Dr. John H. Watson must have felt on an
evening in 1895 as outside the hansoms rattled over cob-
blestones in the rain. The sea coal flames upon the hearth,
and across the room Holmes sits coiled in his armchair, his
haggard and ascetic face hardly visible amid the swirl of
tobacco smoke as he ponders a new problem." He leaned

toward Nick, eyes alight with excitement. "And somewhere out there lurks Moriarty—*plotting*."

Nick grunted. "It isn't raining, there are no hansom cabs, Cambridge streets are asphalt, I have no hearth, this"—he held up his cigar—"is not a pipe, and the year is not 1895."

Woolley sank back in the chair and sighed. "More's the pity!"

The silence that reenveloped them was broken now and again by a little gurgling sound from Woolley's pipe. "That's what comes of not letting a pipe rest between smokes," said Nick, a little irritably. "I thought by now, Professor, that you knew that if you are going out for an evening, you ought to carry two pipes. Better yet, smoke cigars."

"I haven't the right physiognomy for cigars. A pipe suits my profile."

"Then please help yourself to one of my pipe cleaners. That gurgling is driving me nuts."

"What's bothering you is not my pipe, it's the Natalie Goodman case," said Woolley as he reached toward a shelf on which stood a purloined Farley's coffee mug Nick had converted to a pipe-cleaner holder. "If you prefer to ponder it alone, I'll retire and leave you in peace."

"As Holmes once said to Watson, 'I'd be lost without my Boswell.' "

"If that's the case," said Woolley, running the cleaner into the pipe, "I've been thinking."

"Good. Please continue."

"Did Natalie offer an explanation as to why she suspects the people on her list?"

"Only in the sketchiest way. Spurned lover, hurt feelings, resentment of her sticking her nose in their private lives, her need to control, greed."

"All the usual motives."

The phone rang. "It's probably Peg," Nick said, "looking for movie-set gossip."

Instead of Peg's invariably cheery voice, he heard a man's. "Sorry to bother you so late, Mr. Chase. This is Sergeant Granick, Boston Police Department."

"What can I do for you, Sergeant?"

"There's been an incident involving a friend of yours, a Natalie Goodman."

"What kind of incident?"

"A shooting."

"When? Where? How is she?"

"The lady is fine, unhurt but shaken. It appears that somebody took a shot at her as she was returning to her hotel, the Copley Plaza. She would like to speak with you. May I put her on the phone?"

"Of course."

"Just a second."

Woolley was at the edge of his seat. "What's happened?"

"The cops say someone took another shot at Natalie."

She came on the phone. "*Now* do you believe me?"

"Tell me what happened."

"I'd just stepped from a taxi when I heard something whiz past my ear. I thought it was an insect, a bee, perhaps. Then the cab driver began yelling and cursing like a wild man. The bullet had struck the rear window. When police came, they found it lodged in the back of the front seat."

"Have you told the police of the previous attempts?"

"No. I don't want to be delayed in leaving for the island. I go first thing in the morning."

"Will you be traveling alone?"

"Tony's accompanying me. I've arranged for a limo at eight o'clock. A plane service will fly me to Portsmouth. My yacht will take me to the island."

"Here's what I want you to do. Meet me in the lobby at seven. Professor Woolley and I will drive you to the airport in Woolley's car. Tony will take the limo as arranged. Got it?"

"Whatever you say, Nick. And thank you."

"See you in the lobby at seven. And don't tell anyone of this change of plan."

"I'll have to let Tony know."

"You can tell him on your way out the door."

"Surely, you don't suspect that Tony—"

"Seven o'clock sharp, Natalie."

As Nick hung up the phone, Woolley exclaimed, "This is great! The game's afoot again."

"Sorry to have to roust you out of bed so early, my friend," Nick said. "I trust that heap you call a car is gassed up."

"It is indeed."

"It's an early start, so you'd better get to bed."

Perched like a bird at the edge of his chair, Woolley slapped a thigh. "Nick, do you really expect me to be able to sleep?"

Nick laid his cigar in an ashtray. "You may do as you wish. I'm hitting the hay."

Seven

WHEN THE CLOCK radio next to Nick's bed went on, a mellifluous male voice said, "Here are the headlines at six o'clock. Our top story: Boston police say the target of a shooting outside the Copley Plaza late last night appears to have been movie producer Natalie Goodman. She was not hurt and when asked about the incident had no comment. Police say there are no suspects."

Nick grunted. "That's what they think."

"The British prime minister, Tony Blair, says his government remains confident that talks aimed at bringing peace to Northern Ireland are on track."

"Good luck, Tony," said Nick, switching off the radio and going into the bathroom for a daily confrontation with a mirror that reflected the truth of Woolley's unforgiving portrait of him in *Smoking Out a Killer*. He was no longer the flat-bellied, lion-maned, hard NYPD homicide detective with a square no-nonsense jaw. Looking back at him now as he shaved was a grandfatherly proprietor of a tobacco shop in an age of antismoking zealots, who were every bit as militant as Natalie Goodman had been sitting in at the Copley Plaza and making trouble for Richard Nixon.

Now, for some reason, she had become the target of a gunman on the doorstep of that very hotel in the heart of Boston.

Presently, as he put on a tan turtleneck shirt, dark-brown socks and pants, and brown shoes, he heard Woolley moving about in the apartment above and tried to imagine the courtly professor more than quarter of a century younger and afire with the same outrage that had fueled Natalie. Had they been antiwar protesters in New York, he mused, they might have found themselves being arrested by that flat-bellied, lion-maned cop who somewhere, somehow, along the way had been transformed into a widowed and retired detective, owner of The Happy Smoking Ground, proud father of a newspaperman son and a criminologist daughter, and doting grandfather of two.

Fifteen minutes after shaving and dressing, he sat in the chair that Woolley had occupied, eating a honey-glazed doughnut and hearing the professor's footsteps thumping down the stairs. A moment later, the door opened. Dressed in a dark suit, white shirt, and striped tie, as though he had an early seminar to conduct at Harvard, Woolley declared. "Good, you're up."

"I hope you slept well."

"Not a wink."

"There's coffee and doughnuts in the kitchen."

"What sort of breakfast is that?"

"Suit yourself."

"The shooting was on the news on the radio."

"So I've heard."

"You're very blasé about this, Nick," said Woolley, disappearing into the kitchen.

"How should I be?"

Woolley emerged doughnut in hand. "I've been thinking about last night."

"And what have you concluded?"

"It seems to me that whoever fired that shot at Natalie knew she would be going out."

"Why not shoot her then?"

"Perhaps he found he couldn't get a clear shot at that time."

"Possibly."

"So he waited patiently for her to return."

"Now you've put your finger on something significant, Professor," Nick said, lighting the day's first cigar. "The initial try at killing Natalie happened on a freeway. The second was weeks later at her home in the mountains. Even more time elapsed before the next attempts, the falling light of yesterday afternoon and the shot last night. What does the timing suggest?"

Woolley gobbled the remainder of the doughnut. " He's evidently intent on murdering her, yet before yesterday he'd shown very little urgency in trying to do so."

"Exactly," Nick said as he stood and put on a brown-and-white houndstooth jacket. "The timing is determined by his proximity. Time elapsed between the first and second because this would-be assassin didn't have the opportunity to try again immediately. He was somewhere else. Natalie figured out that whoever is trying to kill her is close, but not every day, which is why she's arranged to bring the people she suspects together this weekend. 'Come into my parlor,' said the spider to the fly."

"Audacious of her to set a trap," said Woolley, licking his fingers, "but terribly risky."

"As you pointed out, she's a remarkable woman," Nick said, slipping a leather three-finger cigar case into the inside pocket of his jacket and a snub-nosed .38-caliber Smith & Wesson police special pistol into the right-hand side pocket. "Are you ready to go?"

Unimpeded by the heavy morning traffic they would have faced later, they crossed the Charles River on the Harvard Bridge, proceed along Massachusetts Avenue, turned into Boylston Street, and arrived at Copley Square in front of the hotel at ten minutes to seven.

"I'll get out here," said Nick. "Pull the car into Trinity Place. I don't want to bring Natalie out through the front entrance. You stay by the car with the back door open."

"Ready for a quick getaway, eh?"

"Keep your eye on people on the street."

A moment later, he found Natalie waiting in the lobby, wearing a gray suit and without luggage. "Right on time," she said, looking round nervously.

"No bags?" he asked.

"Tony will bring them in the limo."

"Good."

"He's not at all happy about this abrupt change in plans."

"Somehow I think he'll get over it. Woolley's waiting with the car on Trinity Place. We'll go out through a side door. Stay close but behind me."

Following him across the lobby, she said, "I'll be glad to get out of Boston."

Nick stopped at the door. "Stay here while I check the street." Stepping outside, he saw no one but Woolley.

Standing by the car's opened rear door, Woolley called, "All's clear."

Nick signaled Natalie to exit, and she stepped out.

"By the way," he said as they reached the car, "you're the big story on the news."

"That kind of publicity," she said, ducking into the rear seat, "I can do without."

"You drive, Professor," Nick said, sliding in beside her.

"Good morning, Natalie," Woolley said. "How are you feeling?"

"Like a character in one of my movies."

"No need to worry, my dear," Woolley replied, starting the car. "You're in good hands now, I assure you. Soon you'll be at your island retreat, safe and sound."

"What kind of security do you have there?" Nick asked.

"The usual burglar alarms."

"No guards?"

"I've never felt the need."

"Neighbors?"

"Mine is the only house on the island."

Nick surveyed Copley Square. "How far is it to the nearest house?"

"The closest is on the next island, about two miles."

"What about hired help? Servants?"

"None when I'm not there. I have a caretaker, who lives on another island. He looks in at my place once a week."

"How far to the nearest police station?"

"That would be on the mainland, several miles away."

"It sounds like a pretty damned remote spot," said Woolley.

"That's the idea."

"So it's just you and Tony until the guests arrive Friday evening?" asked Nick as Woolley drove toward an entrance to Storrow Drive.

"A cook and a maid will be there, starting tomorrow."

"Do you keep any guns in the house?"

"As a charter member of an organization that lobbies for gun control," she said, "I'd be a hypocrite if I owned one, wouldn't I?"

With the car moving swiftly along the Charles, Nick asked, "Who knew that you'd be going out for dinner last night?"

"When I travel, I always go out for dinner."

"Did you tell anyone of your plan to have dinner with me?"

"Tony knew, of course."

"Where was Tony when you returned to the hotel?"

"I found him asleep in my suite. Surely, you don't think that he—"

"It's my job to think of every possibility," Nick said. "Who knew you were staying at Copley Plaza?"

"Everyone knows that my preferred hotel when I'm in Boston is the Copley Plaza."

"Who in your organization would know your schedule on any given day?"

"When a film is under way, my schedule is part of the weekly production sheet. It notes where I'll be on what date, phone numbers, and so forth. I try to be accessible to my people."

After a looping route that took them to a tunnel under Boston Harbor, they arrived at the airport at seven-thirty. "Might I suggest, because we have time before Tony arrives," said Nick, "that we grab breakfast?"

"Capital idea," asserted Woolley.

An hour later the limousine pulled up, and fifteen minutes later Natalie was airborne.

Watching the plane ascend, Woolley asked, "Do you think she'll be safe?"

"Oh, yes," said Nick, taking out a cigar and a box of matches.

"Good lord, man," exclaimed Woolley. "Don't you know it's dangerous to light up on an airfield? Do you want us to go up in a ball of exploding fumes?"

PART III

North from Boston

Eight

"YOU MAY CALL me a cynical newspaperman," declared Kevin Chase on Thursday evening as his wife Noreen emerged from the kitchen with a pot of coffee to complete their dinner, "but all this smacks of a movie publicity stunt."

"A mighty dangerous one," said Noreen, filling Nick's cup. "I examined the bullet that was fired through that cab window. If Natalie Goodman had still been in the backseat, it would have been fatal."

"But she wasn't in the backseat, was she? That shot missed her by a country mile."

"The incident report filed by Sergeant Granick says it was less than two feet."

Nick lit a small cigar. "What was it Churchill said about being shot at? Something to the effect that there is no experience quite so gratifying as a bullet fired at you without effect." He smiled at his daughter-in-law. "Noreen, my compliments on another of your excellent dinners. I'm sorry the kids couldn't join us."

"You know about teenagers," she said, pouring coffee for Kevin. "On Thursday evenings they hang out with their friends at the mall."

"In my day we loitered in front of old man Fulmer's corner cigar store. I suppose that's why I went into the tobacco business after I retired and Maggie died. I'm harking back to the halcyon days of my youth."

Kevin shifted impatiently in his chair. "This is another of your slick attempts to avoid the subject at hand."

"What subject am I attempting to avoid?"

"This cock-and-bull story that woman's been handing you about her life being in danger."

"I've told you this in confidence, Kevin. It's off the record. I don't want to read all about it in your newspaper."

"Don't worry. I'm not interested in participating in a hoax aimed at drumming up publicity for a movie."

"That's ridiculous," said Noreen, resuming her place at the table. "The picture's only just begun production. It will be months, maybe a year, before it's released."

"Noreen makes a good point," said Nick. "If *Smoking Out a Killer* were finished and about to be released, then I might also be skeptical about these reported attempts on Natalie Goodman's life."

"Ah ha! You said 'reported attempts.' If someone's trying to kill her, where are the witnesses? Where's her evidence?"

"I'm a witness. Before the incident with the taxi someone took a shot at her as she and I were leaving Farley's. That's off the record, Kevin."

"Both shots were part of the publicity ploy. I still say it smells like a scheme to involve the man on whom the movie is based in a publicity gimmick. If Natalie believes someone's out to kill her, it's a matter for the police, not an occasion for a weekend get-together on an island. I'm sorry to say it, Dad, but I think you're being hoodwinked."

Nick admired the even burn of the cigar. "As long as there is a possibility that Natalie's life is at stake and I can do something about it, I have to take that chance."

"At least you're going to her island in grand style," said Noreen dreamily. "I think yachts are so . . . romantic!"

"The whole thing sounds like a plot in one of Professor Woolley's books," Kevin said, forcefully. "I wouldn't be at all surprised if Woolley and Goodman were in cahoots in this."

Nick smiled. "Were Woolley here, I'm sure he'd take that remark as a compliment."

"He's always been a schemer of the first rank. Just because he's now a senior citizen and a best-selling author doesn't mean he's mended his ways. He's got a history with Goodman. I pulled the news clips from their days as anti-war radicals. He was a ringleader. He planned that famous sit-in at the Copley Plaza."

Nick puffed the cigar. "There's no question that he's still got the spark of adventure, but involve me in a plot with Natalie for a publicity stunt? I don't think so."

"More coffee, Nick?" Noreen asked.

"No, thanks, my dear. I should be going. It's getting close to my bedtime. And I've got a long day ahead of me tomorrow. The *Murder Two* casts off at ten A.M. sharp."

Nine

As NICK DROVE from his son's home in Brookline, those who would be joining him in the morning at Rowes Wharf were either in Boston or en route.

The memorandums on New Millennium Films letterhead informing them that they were expected to come to Pirate's Cove Island had been sent by fax or FedEx or were delivered by a messenger.

Without a salutation, it was not an invitation, but a command:

> Imperative that you come to my summer home on Pirate's Cove Island for the weekend following completion of initial shooting in Cambridge. Vital business to discuss, followed by ample time for relaxation in the sun and soft ocean breezes. Exquisite food and plenty to drink. Delightful companionship and unique entertainment. My yacht departs Rowes Wharf, Boston, at 10 A.M. Friday, the 12th and returns on the 15th. I know you won't disappoint me.
>
> N.G.

Rather than receiving separate notifications, Harry Hardin and Sheila Stevens had found one addressed to both of them and slipped under the door of Harry's Copley Plaza suite.

Written in Natalie's hand at the bottom was, "For appearances's sake, you will be assigned separate rooms, but you'll find they have a connecting door. Meantime, you may remain in your present accommodations at the company's expense, but please be discreet."

"What a snide bitch," seethed Sheila as she sat nude in front of a dressing table mirror and read the memo. "And damned rude on top of it. Well, to hell with her, I'm not going."

Harry bent, brushed aside her long hair, and nibbled the back of her neck "Of course you are. You're as curious as I am to find out what she's up to."

"I wouldn't put it past her to conceal a video camera in each of our rooms."

Harry chuckled. "Perhaps she'll run a certain porno tape for the guests after dinner. That may be what she means by 'unique entertainment.' "

Sheila crumpled the memo and flung it to the floor.

Harry turned and sprawled naked on the bed. "Come on, Sheel, lighten up. It will probably turn out to be a fun weekend. Natalie may be a bitch, but she knows how to throw a party."

Sheila spoke to his reflection in the mirror. "Who else do you suppose she's invited?"

"Who cares? We'll have each other, right? I think her assigning us rooms with a connecting door is very sweet of her."

"Joke all you like," she said, leaving the dresser for the bed, "But I don't like this weekend thing, Harry. I really have a bad feeling about it."

Unsettled, too, had been Simon Cane, Esquire, Attorney-at-Law. At nine o'clock Monday morning his secretary had placed the fax on his large desk in a spacious corner suite on the thirty-fourth floor of the Helmsley Building astride Park Avenue at Forty-sixth Street in New York City. At the bottom of the memo, Natalie had inscribed, "I know you were planning to come up to Pirate's Cove on the Saturday after the first day's shooting in Cambridge, dear Simon, but you must be here Friday. Do forgive the inconvenience. This is a matter of utmost urgency."

And damned inconvenient it would be. To leave Boston at ten in the morning meant an eight o'clock flight on Friday and canceling a day of pretrial conferences in the delicate matter of Wieser vs. Morris, docketed to go to trial with jury selection in the federal district court at Foley Square on Monday. Now someone else would have to handle the conferences and, in all likelihood, if he could not arrange a flight back to New York on Sunday, start the voir dire.

In an attempt to persuade Natalie to allow him to come to the island Saturday as planned, he'd placed a call to her at the Copley Plaza. "Natalie," he pleaded, "must we all be there? How can it possibly matter if I come up a day later?"

"I need you there on Friday. It matters a great deal to both our futures," she said icily. "I expect you to be there as arranged. It's a casual occasion, by the way. So leave your pinstripe, double-breasted courtroom attire at home. I know you enjoy dressing for dinner, but no tuxedos either, darling."

It was not until well past noon in Westhampton, Long Island, when Richard Edwards felt an urgent call of nature and left Parker Slade sleeping in splendid full arousal in the master bedroom of his mansion, that he noticed a FedEx envelope had been passed under the door by the security service. Standing at the toilet, he read the typed text and a handwritten notation at the bottom. "I trust you will bring your dear friend Parker—no, I insist that he come. I like him very much. We have much to talk about."

Returning to the bedroom, Richard shook the handsome youth awake.

Parker stirred, gripped his erection, and smiled sweetly. "Wha' time's it?"

"I have good news and bad news, lover. The good part is that I've been ordered to bring you along for an entire weekend with Natalie. She likes you very much."

"Swell," Parker said. "What's the bad?"

"Alas," Richard answered as he settled onto the bed. "The trip to Paris that we were to take that weekend will have to be postponed."

"For how long?"

"That, my dear," Richard said, kissing Parker's flat belly, "is entirely up to Natalie."

At the same time in Malibu, California, Nigel Wilson's memo had also arrived by FedEx. Handed to him by his valet at the end of a daily workout, Nigel looked at the name of the sender, grimaced, tore open the red-white-and-blue envelope, read the contents, and turned to his training partner, Clifford Branson.

"I have been ordered by the Wicked Witch of the West to drop everything and join her and god knows who else for an entire weekend on her hideous island."

Dabbing his sweaty forehead with a towel, Clifford said, "I hate that place."

"Be that as it may, there is vital business to be done."

"Maybe she's decided to exercise her option and buy you out."

Clifford's eyes narrowed to slits. "Very funny indeed!"

An hour and a half later, when Branson arrived at the New Millennium Films offices at Century City in Los Angeles, the receptionist handed him his own faxed memo. On the phone immediately to Nigel, he said, "I've also been invited to the island."

"Naturally you have. We'll go together. I really detest flying alone."

Ten

BARGING INTO NICK'S apartment at nine o'clock Friday morning, Woolley carried a purple duffle bag and sported a white captain's hat with a gold anchor, navy-blue double-breasted jacket over a wide-waled white turtleneck shirt, duck trousers, and brown gum-soled deck shoes.

Nick looked up from a breakfast of toast and coffee. "Where'd you find that getup?"

Woolley closed the door and set the bag next to it. "One can't have lived in New England as long as I have and not been invited to go sailing on occasion. I passed many a summer hiatus from Harvard in the Barnstable oceanside cottage of Jerome Lazarus, of late and dubious memory." He peered disapprovingly at Nick's attire of brown-and-white houndstooth jacket, tan pullover shirt, chocolate pants, and brown-and-white saddle shoes. "You are not wearing those duds? We're going yachting, not golfing. Have you nothing of a seafaring nature?"

"The closest I ever came to faring the sea," said Nick, carrying his coffee mug and a plate into the kitchen, "was taking the Staten Island ferry to the scene of an axe murder, and, once, a Circle Line boat ride around Manhattan to entertain visiting in-laws."

"I've called a cab to take us to the wharf. It should be here in a few minutes. The weather man on the radio forecasts a perfect day for our voyage. Warm, clear skies, and smooth sailing."

"Good."

"It's funny that you should mention an axe murder," Woolley said, standing in the kitchen doorway as Nick rinsed his cup. "There was just such an atrocity committed over a hundred years ago on one of the Isles of Shoals, which are our destination today."

"Always the historian of crime," said Nick as the cup went upside down into a dish drainer.

"An immigrant fisherman hacked two women to death and severely wounded another in a failed attempt at robbery on Smutty Nose Island."

Nick dried his hands. "Smutty Nose. What a name."

"I'm counting on having time this weekend for me to pay a visit to the murder scene," Woolley said, stepping aside to let Nick leave the kitchen. "I hope you'll accompany me."

"I've seen quite enough murder scenes in my lifetime, Professor," Nick said, picking up a battered suitcase. "I've no interest in visiting hundred-year-old ones."

Woolley retrieved his duffle bag. "It was a very famous murder, a sensational trial, and a hanging, of course."

Nick closed and locked the door. Going down the stairs, he said, "I've got to duck into the store for a minute. Natalie expects me to entertain after dinner by talking about cigars, so I'd better take an assortment with me. I trust you're well stocked with pipe tobacco? There's nothing more calamitous for a gentleman who smokes than suddenly discovering that he's gone and run out of ammunition."

Woolley patted the duffle bag. "I'm fully prepared."

When Nick came out of the store carrying several cigar boxes in a shopping bag, he found the taxi waiting.

"Ah, soon we will be under way," exclaimed Woolley as they settled in the back of the cab. "In the words of the nineteenth-century poet Thomas Lovell Beddoes:

The anchor heaves, the ship swings free,
The sails swell full. To sea, to sea!"

"Very nice, professor, but the *Murder Two* is a motor yacht."

Woolley sighed. "At times like this I regret having been born in the twentieth century. I suppose that's why I've so enjoyed living in Cambridge. Thus far, at least, the town has shunned the urge of the city across the Charles River to tear down the old to make way for the atrocities of steel and glass in the graceless towers that now dominate the downtown area and waterfront. I miss the red brick of the old Boston. Admit it, Nicholas, wouldn't you rather being heading north from Boston aboard a ship in full sail?"

"If I have to go to sea," Nick replied as the taxi dashed along Massachusetts Avenue, "I prefer to do so in a vessel with ship-to-shore radio, radar, a well-equipped galley, nicely stocked bar, and a head that has a flush toilet."

"Creature comforts! Where's your sense of adventure, man?"

"Being asked to unmask a would-be murderer doesn't qualify as an adventure?"

"Yes, of course, but, well, you know what I mean."

Nick patted Woolley's knee. "You go ahead and indulge your romanticism, my friend, but don't let it get in the way of your duty. I'll be relying on you to help me sort out the characters Natalie Goodman has cast in the leading roles of this melodrama she's scripted."

"Except for the ending, of course. Nick Chase will write that."

"My son thinks I'm being hoodwinked."

Woolley looked at Nick with amazement. "In what way?"

"Kevin's opinion is that Natalie is orchestrating an elaborate stunt to generate publicity for the movie."

"Utter nonsense. She's been attacked five times."

"And survived them all, Kevin points out."

"Excuse my bluntness, Nick, but Kevin is a member of a generation which finds a conspiracy in everything that's happened since the assassination of John F. Kennedy and a large segment of which believes the government is covering up that Earth is being visited regularly by creatures from outer space. I believe that someone has been trying to kill Natalie, and so do you, obviously, or you wouldn't be undertaking this excursion and leaving the running of The Happy Smoking Ground on a busy weekend to an underling."

"If I were you, Professor, I wouldn't call Craig Spencer an underling to his face."

"You know exactly what I'm getting at, Nick. That you've left the store for three days means you regard this matter with utmost gravity."

As the cab darted across Harvard Bridge, Nick looked left to peer through the window in the direction of Esplanade, where he attended summer concerts by the Boston Pops orchestra at the Hatch Memorial shell. Sailboats dotted the calm surface of the Charles River under a cloudless August sky that formed a blue backdrop for the gleaming towers of the new Boston that the elderly man in the yachting togs disdained.

Turning to Woolley, he said, "There is nothing graver than murder, Professor."

Eleven

SINCE EIGHT O'CLOCK, Ivo Bogdanovich had been getting a crash course in how to be a deck hand from the skipper of *Murder Two*. A muscular youth with the chiseled looks of a movie star, Dave Kolker had short black hair, a handsome, angular face, strong arms, and powerful legs. Taut skin burnished by hours in the sun made a snug T-shirt and hip-hugging shorts seem whiter than white. With astonishing patience he had taught Ivo that when the boat was about to get under way, his job was to free various ropes and cables and either pull them into the boat or fling them onto the dock.

"That's what's meant by casting off," Dave had explained. "Once we've cleared the harbor and are at cruising speed, and until we get to Pirate's Cove Island, your main duty will be to see to the passengers. That will mostly involve serving them drinks. There will be a bartender, so you won't have to mix them. He'll also handle the buffet lunch. His name is Bill Restivo."

Boarding at nine o'clock carrying a small weekend bag and wearing a short white waiter's jacket and tuxedo shirt with black bow tie and white pants, Restivo was tall and rangy with the quick, wanting-to-please smile of an actor at an audition, which this job was, or so he had been told when Tony Biciano had hired him.

"Natalie was impressed by the way you handled the catering of Richard Edwards's birthday party in Westhampton," Tony had said, "and I'm pretty sure that if you handle this little job as you did that one, I can persuade Natalie to reward you not only financially, but with a small speaking part in *Smoking Out a Killer*."

With Ivo and Bill aboard, Dave had provided a tour of the seventy-eight-foot yacht's three decks. The topmost was a flybridge. Below, the main deck had a spacious area with a four-seat couch at the stern and a sumptuous interior lounge with two facing built-in sofas, an oval dining table seating eight, a small bar, compact galley, and a head. Forward and two steps up was the cockpit with a wraparound windscreen. A spiral stair led below to quarters accommodating four people in two snug cabins with single bunks, a roomy forward cabin with a double bed, and spacious master suite amidships. Immediately aft of this, behind a soundproof wall, was the engine room with two 1,350-horsepower diesel motors capable of producing a cruising speed of twenty-six knots. Aft of the engine room on the port side were quarters for two crewmen.

By nine-thirty, *Murder Two*, skipper Kolker, Ivo, and Bill were ready to welcome aboard the nine guests for a leisurely northeasterly coast-hugging voyage past quaint old fishing towns of the North Shore. Going around Cape Ann, they would head east of Portsmouth, New Hampshire, to the Isles of Shoals. A little beyond them lay Pirate's Cove Island. If all went as charted, they'd arrive in time for cocktails before dinner.

Looking at the yacht from a window booth in the coffee shop of the Boston Harbor Hotel at Rowes Wharf, Harry Hardin shook his head slowly and said to Sheila Stevens, "You've gotta hand it to Natalie, she really knows how to go first class. What do you suppose that boat cost?"

"I'm sure it was much less than what you're getting to star in her film," said Sheila, "not counting your two percent of gross."

"As you know, darling, the term 'gross' is very elastic.

But if your showing all this interest in what I'm earning anticipates a possible future divorce settlement, you're dreaming. If we ever tie the knot, there'll be a prenuptial agreement as ironclad as Simon Cane can make it."

"Isn't it a conflict of interest for him to be representing both you and Natalie on this film?"

"What do I care? He got me a very good deal."

"And a hell of a nice one for himself, I'd say. Fifteen percent of you and lord knows what he's squeezing out of Natalie."

"You haven't done badly. I happen to know how much you're being paid, whether your script is used or not." Turning to the window, he exclaimed, "Well, the weekend won't be a total loss. Look who just showed up."

Sheila observed two men stepping from a taxi. "Am I supposed to know those guys?"

"The gentleman in the blue blazer wrote the book you adapted. The other is the real-life inspiration for its main character. Suddenly the prospects for this weekend have gotten a whole lot brighter. C'mon, let's join them."

As Ivo took Nick's bags and Woolley's duffle, Nick said, "You're obviously a man of many talents, Ivo. First a location scout, then all-round assistant on the set, and now you're an able-bodied sailor."

Ivo beamed. "And baggage handler. Welcome aboard, Nick. If there's anything I can do to make you and Mr. Woolley more comfortable, just give me a shout."

"Who else has arrived?"

"You and Mr. Woolley are the first. The captain is Dave Kolker. And there's a bartender named Bill. Would you care to go into the lounge, or do you prefer the back of the boat?"

"It's not the back," said Woolley, "it's the stern."

Ivo looked him up and down. "I didn't know you were you a sailing man, Mr. Woolley."

Nick chuckled. "Only in his heart, Ivo. We'll sit at the back."

"May I bring you something to drink?"

"Capital idea," exclaimed Woolley. "Make mine a gin and tonic."

"And you, Nick?"

"None for me, Ivo. I never drink till the sun's over the yardarm."

The youth looked puzzled. "Beg pardon?"

"I'll have something a little later."

As he spoke, Harry Hardin bounded aboard.

"Ahoy, Nick. What ho, Woolley," he shouted, throwing them a smart salute. Turning, he assisted Sheila from dock to deck. Tall and willowy with short blond hair, she carried a large straw bag and wore a loose denim shirt with the tail out, white jeans, and gray tennis shoes. "This is Sheila Stevens," Harry declared, "the gal who wrote the script."

She and Woolley sat on the couch. Nick and Harry leaned against a rail facing the dock.

"You have no idea how glad I am to see you, Nick," said Harry. "Suddenly, this weekend has taken on a whole new dimension. I was resigned to three nights and two days of nothing but shop talk. You have no idea how boring movie people can be. All they know or care about is the film industry. With you and Woolley joining Natalie's flock, the conversation promises to be a lot more interesting. I've never known a detective. I'm looking forward to hearing about your cases."

"Gosh, I was hoping to hear exciting Hollywood stories."

As a white stretch limo glided to stop next to the yacht, Harry let out a groan. "Oh, hell, it's Nigel Wilson and Cliff Branson." Casually dressed and carrying medium-sized gym bags, the two men were welcomed aboard by Ivo and escorted directly into the lounge. "If I'd have known they were joining this junket," Harry continued sourly, "I'd have sent Natalie my regrets. They are the personification of what I was saying about film folks. All they ever want to talk about is the business."

"I understood that Natalie had fired Branson."

"That's the film biz, Nick. Fired today, rehired tomorrow."

A few minutes later, Simon Cane strode across the wharf.

* * *

Getting to Boston in time had been a close thing. Just as he was leaving his house, he'd gotten a phone call from Nigel Wilson that held him up for ten minutes. Then the plane had been half an hour late leaving the gate and had sat for another fifteen minutes waiting clearance for takeoff.

"Welcome aboard, sir," said Ivo cheerily as he reached for the lawyer's suitcase.

Cane made a slight bow in the direction of the foursome at the stern. "How many others are expected?"

"There will be nine in all, sir, counting you."

"Are they all here?"

"All but Mr. Edwards and Parker Slade."

"Show me where I can freshen up."

As Ivo and Cane disappeared, Woolley took a sip of gin and tonic and turned slightly to Sheila Stevens. "As a writer, Miss Stevens, what sort of motion picture would you make out of this situation? Might all these people be characters in a drama? A romantic comedy? A murder yarn, perhaps? Or would you go for a life-and-death struggle as a ship goes down at sea?"

"They've already done that one, Professor," interjected Nick as he and Harry joined Woolley and Sheila on the couch. "It was an Alfred Hitchcock production starring Tallulah Bankhead and John Hodiak called *Lifeboat*."

Harry barked a laugh. "Ah, Nick, you are such a tease."

"Why? It was an excellent movie."

"We expected you to name *Titanic*."

"Sorry. I haven't seen it."

"You must be the only person who hasn't."

"The story of the *Titanic* was told very well in *A Night to Remember*. My late wife and I saw it at Radio City Music Hall, I believe."

"Tell me, Miss Stevens," said Woolley eagerly. "How do you know if you've written a good screenplay?"

"I usually regard my latest work as the worst script ever written—unless Tom Cruise or Harry Hardin want to do it."

"If I were in your profession," Woolley said, "and I had been asked to write a screenplay incorporating a small group of people such as ourselves thrown together aboard a boat, I'd take the murder-mystery route. It certainly paid off for Agatha Christie in *Death on the Nile, Ten Little Indians,* and even *Murder on the Orient Express,* which begins on a ferryboat. However, my favorite mystery-on-a-boat movie is *Pursuit to Algiers,* with Basil Rathbone as Sherlock Holmes. Nigel Bruce as Dr. Watson sings 'Loch Lomond,' and rather delightfully. It's a story not written by Sir Arthur Conan Doyle or even based on one of his yarns." He glanced at Nick. "Holmes's task was not to solve a murder, but prevent one."

Gazing forward, Nick watched a young man in white T-shirt and shorts emerge from the cabin. "I presume this is our skipper."

"Excuse me, folks," said Dave Kolker. "I just wanted to let you know that we'll be a little late departing. I've had a phone call from Mr. Edwards. He and Mr. Slade are on their way and should be here in ten or fifteen minutes."

Harry grunted. "That's typical. No doubt Rich felt he had to get in one more roll in the hay with the kid, and the rest of us be damned."

"As soon as they're aboard, we'll set sail," said Kolker. "There'll be a buffet lunch available at noon, but the bar is open now. Ivo will be happy to serve you. One more thing. The law requires that you wear life jackets. You'll find four under the seats of the couch. They're easy to put on, but if you have any trouble, I'll be glad to assist."

Nick asked, "What's the estimated time of arrival at Pirate's Cove?"

"We should be dockside at the island at four-thirty, five at the latest."

"Assuming," said Harry, "that the overdue lovers can tear themselves apart."

Sheila frowned. "I understand why Rich would be summoned, but why would Natalie include Parker Slade?"

"Invite you, you get me. Invite Rich Edwards, you also must invite the kid."

"Excuse me, Sheila," Nick said. "Why did you say 'summoned' rather than 'invited?' "

Sheila dug into her bag, withdrew Natalie's memo, and handed it to Nick. "How would you interpret the word 'imperative?' "

Nick read the message quickly, noted the postscript concerning connecting rooms, and returned it. "Natalie is not a woman who minces her words, obviously."

Harry Hardin smiled. "I hope she was more charming in wording your invitation, Nick."

"Mine was verbal, actually. And a request, not an order."

Sheila stuffed the memo into the bag. "That's only because you're not on her payroll."

"Have you any idea what business she wants to discuss that's so vital?"

"Since she's summoned Cliff Branson back from Siberia," Harry said, encircling Sheila's shoulder with an arm, "perhaps she's decided to revamp the entire production, starting with a rewrite of the script."

"Natalie can do what she wishes," Sheila replied, shrugging off the arm. "I get paid no matter what she does with my screenplay. One thing that she can't change, however, is the star, so you can rest easy, Harry."

"I could quit."

"Natalie would still come out a winner, wouldn't she? How long would it take after you walked off the picture for her to collect on the completion insurance policy she took out and then for Simon Cane to slap you with a breach of contract lawsuit?"

"That would be interesting," Harry said with a laugh. "Simon Cane would be suing one client on behalf of another!" He looked at Nick. "You see what I mean about movie people? All we ever talk about is the business. I'm afraid you may be in for a boring weekend, my friend. Of course, Natalie did promise us some unique entertainment, whatever that means."

"It means me," Nick replied. "Natalie has asked me to be an after-dinner speaker."

"Marvelous! What's the subject, Nick Chase's greatest cases?"

Nick peered past Harry to observe the arrival of two men he assumed to be Edwards and Slade. "I'm going to tell you more than you probably care to know about cigars."

Twelve

WITH THE LAST of the passengers aboard, there was a flurry of activity on the part of Ivo Bogdanovich concerning ropes and lines, a gurgling of water, and an almost imperceptible hum of engines as *Murder Two* eased away from Rowes Wharf.

Leaving Woolley with Harry Hardin and Sheila Stevens, Nick passed wordlessly through the lounge, acutely conscious of being observed by the passengers, and went up the two steps into the cockpit. Dave Kolker sat in a high-backed upholstered armchair, suntanned hands on a small wheel, facing a crescent-shaped control console and instrument panel.

"Do you mind if I look over your shoulder, Captain?"

"Not at all, sir."

"She's quite a ship."

"Very yare."

"How long have you been at her helm?"

"She's brand spanking new. Built in the Turinese boatyard. That's in Italy."

"I know."

"Yes, of course. Before *Murder Two*, Mrs. Goodman had a much smaller craft, which I ran for her between Portsmouth and Pirate's Cove and sometimes down to Boston. She's had this one a year but hasn't used her much. Mrs.

Goodman's been on the West Coast most of that time."

Off the port side planes were landing and taking off at Logan International Airport. Off to starboard passed a comparatively ungainly-looking passenger ferry making for Boston.

"She's inbound from Cape Cod," said Kolker, "probably out of Provincetown."

"What course have you chosen for us?"

"When we clear the inner harbor, we turn slightly southeasterly. We sail between the navigational lights of Deer and Long Island and into the Atlantic. Then I set the automatic pilot for a straight course to East Point, Nahant, and on to Tinker's Island and Marblehead Neck. We pass between them. Beyond Cape Ann we turn east over open ocean to the island, about twelve miles out from Portsmouth."

"It seems like a lot of boat for one man to handle."

"She practically sails herself. It's a fairly short and easy day trip."

"I couldn't help but notice that your deck hand today is one of the young men from the movie crew."

"If this were a longer cruise, say down to the Caribbean, there'd be two crewmen. But the guys I'd usually bring on board weren't available on short notice. This was a last-minute thing. Mrs. Goodman called me about it a couple of days ago. Fortunately, Ivo's a quick learner."

"How is Natalie Goodman as a boss? I hear she can be pretty tough to work for."

"She's always been pleasant with me."

"Do you live on Pirate's Cove Island?"

"Only when Mrs. Goodman is using the yacht, but that's so infrequently that *Murder Two* might as well be mine. Most of the time she's berthed at Portsmouth."

"What do you do when she's not in use?"

"I've got a blues band. I play guitar, sing, write some of the songs."

"When I lived in New York, I used to haunt blues clubs. But that was a long time ago."

Woolley stepped into the cockpit. "Ah, here you are,

Nick. I was beginning to think you'd fallen overboard.
Everybody's having a good time on the after deck, and
there's a distinct feeling among them that you're not very
sociable."

"Thanks for the hospitality, Captain."

"In other words," said Nick to Woolley with a nod toward the bartender as he followed Woolley through the
otherwise unoccupied lounge, "our shipmates are wondering what the hell I'm doing here. What have you told
them?"

"Other than we were invited for the weekend, not a
thing."

"What have they been saying about the shots fired at
Natalie Sunday night?"

"So far, the subject hasn't come up."

"That's interesting," Nick said, coming out on deck.
"Very interesting indeed."

Wordless and facing the diminishing Boston skyline,
their backs toward Nick, the seven guests who had been
summoned to spend a weekend on Natalie Goodman's island appeared to Nick to be actors arrayed on a set and
waiting for a director to shout, "Action!"

Instead, they heard, "What a spectacular view!"

Harry Hardin turned and exclaimed, "Ah, Nick! Allow
me to present the cast."

While he performed the introductions—and that's what
it was, Nick thought: a flawless performance by a consum-
mate actor—Nick did what he'd been so good at as a detective. Instant assessments. Off-the-top-of-the-head
judgments. Gut instinct. Firmness of handshake. Dry palm
or too moist? Directness of eyes, windows of the soul, sup-
posedly. Sincerity of smile. Tone of voice. Overall body
language. Tense? Relaxed? Assertive? Reticent? Suspicious? Bold? Shy? Cunning? Coy? Leader or follower? Capable of premeditated murder? A worthy accomplice?

What was there about the seven guests aboard *Murder
Two*, Nick asked himself as he met them against the background of the receding Boston skyline, that had persuaded

Natalie that one or possibly more of them had the capability and the motivation to kill her?

Harry Hardin, smooth as silk and ruggedly handsome. Actor at the top of a game that had never been for the faint of heart. The winning personality whose name on a contract evidently ensured a film's success as measured by box office receipts. A superstar whose name alone drew financial backing for a project, defined in Hollywood's lexicon as "bankable." Why might Harry be a suspect? Was he having second thoughts about playing Rick Gordon and saw no way to get out of making the picture short of murdering the producer?

Sheila Stevens. Harry's lover, she had the looks and body of a movie star yet chose to write films rather than be in them. Why should Natalie suspect Sheila? Did Natalie see her as Harry's helper? Or was there lurking behind the azure bedroom eyes a motive of her own? Might Sheila kill to keep from being replaced?

Nigel Wilson. Natalie's former lover with aspirations to become a Hollywood mover and shaker in his own right. The drive certainly was there, Nick decided, but did this middle-aged man of wealth and an iron handshake, who evidently worked very hard to tone his body, have the steel backbone required to commit murder?

Clifford Branson. Natalie had fired him as the writer of *Smoking Out a Killer*. Was loss of a screen credit sufficient motive to kill? He and Nigel Wilson had arrived together. Were they conspirators in a murder plot?

Richard Edwards. As Natalie's designated heir to control New Millennium Films, he had a classic motive. But had his undisguised sexual relationship with handsome Parker Slade made him impatient to accelerate receipt of his legacy? Or had Parker Slade acted to take the matter into his own hands?

Simon Cane, lawyer. Firm handshake. Direct look. Self-confident. The only man on board wearing cuff links. Legal advisor and confidant. Might the briefcase he'd carried aboard contain a motive for murder?

These impressions of Natalie's guests were garnered in

a few seconds. They were but snapshots to be reviewed, reassessed, questioned, and either confirmed or rejected on the basis of evidence.

Coming up with a viable suspect was like falling in love. Sometimes it happened at first sight. Usually, you needed time.

PART IV

All at Sea

Thirteen

WITH THE LIGHTHOUSE at Marblehead slipping fast from view, Ivo Bogdanovich emerged from the lounge onto the after deck in noonday sun and announced that a buffet lunch was ready.

"Capital!" said Woolley. "There's nothing like ocean air to whet one's appetite."

Laid out on the dining table in the lounge, lunch consisted of chunks of cold lobster; iced shrimp; thinly sliced salmon; combination seafood, three-bean, greens, and potato salads; thick-sliced tomatoes and onions; cole slaw; fried chicken; Boston baked beans; stacks of overstuffed sandwiches; an assortment of fruits; cake and cookies for dessert; and silver pots of coffee. The wines were Chablis and Burgundy.

"Say what you will about Natalie," said Shelia Stevens to Nick as she surveyed the table, "she'll never let you go away hungry."

Harry Hardin piled a china plate with lobster and shrimp, flashed his multi-million-dollar smile benevolently at Nick, and said, "No one will be able to say that the condemned did not eat a hearty last meal."

Nick chose the combination seafood and a dollop of potato salad. "Condemned? What's that supposed to mean?"

"Pay no attention to Harry," Sheila said sternly as she

carried away a plate of salmon and onions. "Harry is in a Hamlet mood. Like the melancholy prince he longs to play someday on Broadway, he thinks he smells something rotten in Denmark, read that Natalie-land."

"I don't think something's rotten," Harry said, adding a slice of salmon to his plate. "I know it." His voice went to a whisper. "I've been giving a lot of thought to why we've all been commanded into her majesty's presence." He looked around as others entered the lounge. "Let's go below, shall we?"

Nick followed him down a spiral stairway.

Finding the door to a cabin locked, Harry pressed an ear to it and whispered, "Occupied. We'll try the master suite."

Entering it, Harry found himself facing a king-size bed with pink satin sheets at the center of a spacious wood-paneled room with a vanity table and mirror on the starboard side and a broad window seat on the port. He let out a low whistle. "This is really luxurious."

Harry plopped onto the window seat. "Natalie always goes first class. If she knew we were in here, she'd have a fit."

Nick sat on the end of the bed with his plate resting on a knee. "You were saying about the condemned?"

"Trust me, Nick," Harry whispered. "Someone's going to be fired. Canned. Made redundant, as the English say. Cashiered. Axed in full public view. It's Natalie's way. Humiliate and dismiss. In case you haven't noticed—and why on earth should you?—the picture is in trouble. I feel bad for Sheila, I truly do."

"Sheila's going to be fired? I thought she and Natalie were friends."

"Their friendship, such as it is, has nothing to do with it. Sheila has been chosen to be the scapegoat. It's true, she has written a terrible screenplay, but that's not the reason Sheila's head is on the block. I've seen it coming for weeks. I wish there was something I could do to prevent it. What I'm going to say is going to sound terrible, but I regret that whoever fired at Natalie on Sunday night wasn't a better shot."

"Wouldn't that have forced the end of production?"

"Oh, no. Rich Edwards would take over. He should have been in charge from the start. If he had been, the production wouldn't be way over budget. Of course, Natalie would never accept the blame. Natalie always finds some way to save face. In this case, it's poor Sheila."

"Does Sheila know?"

"She certainly suspected. But I don't think she believed it until today when Cliff Branson appeared so dramatically."

"If Natalie is concerned with saving face, why is she bringing back a writer she fired?"

"I would venture, and this is guesswork, that it's Nigel Wilson's doing. You'll note that he and Cliff arrived together."

"Excuse me for being blunt, Harry. It's the detective in me. But do you happen to know where Sheila was on Sunday night?"

"If you're wondering if she shot at Natalie," Harry replied, turning his attention to his lunch, "she definitely has an alibi."

"How do you know?"

Harry chewed a piece of lobster. "Damn, this is good!"

"Sheila's alibi?"

Harry swallowed. "She was with me at the time. We were, if you'll pardon the language, screwing like champions all evening."

Nick cracked a smile. "There were no witnesses, I suppose?"

"I am able to provide a very convincing love scene in the nude in front of a camera with a director, dozens of stage hands, and others looking on," Harry replied with a proud smile, "but when I screw on my own time, it is not my custom to invite an audience."

"Do you have any idea who might have shot at Natalie?"

Harry speared another chunk of lobster with a fork. "If you're looking for suspects—"

"Why would I be looking for suspects?"

"Well, you are a detective."

"I retired long ago. These days I peddle tobacco."

"That didn't stop you from solving the case that's the subject of this movie."

"That was a fluke, I assure you."

"Your interest in who took a pop at Natalie is strictly . . . intellectual?"

"Exactly."

"If you were a practicing detective," Harry said, lifting the lobster to his lips, "I'd advise you to check for suspects in the credits of any of Natalie's films. But for starters, you wouldn't be amiss in taking a look at the passengers on this yacht, excluding yourself and Professor Woolley, of course." He chewed the lobster, swallowed, and smiled. "On second thought, maybe you ought to include Woolley. He wouldn't be the first author of a book who got it into his head to kill the producer who acquired the film rights!"

Fourteen

WHEN NICK AND Harry returned to the lounge, they found a crowd around the dining table. Woolley was standing at the bar as Bill Restivo served him a gin and tonic. A tap on the shoulder by Nick turned Woolley around.

Scowling, he asserted, "You have a maddening talent for disappearing."

"For the record, Professor," said Harry, "where were you last Sunday night?"

Woolley picked up a swizzle stick and stirred the drink. "Why do you ask?"

Nick answered, "Harry thinks you might be the person who fired shots at Natalie."

"What impertinence."

Restivo asked, "What can I get you gentlemen?"

"Scotch neat," said Nick.

"Vodka and tonic," said Harry.

"You know damn well where I was, Nick," Woolley said. "You and I were smoking in your apartment at the time."

"Ah, yes," said Nick as Restivo poured the scotch, "that's right."

Harry offered a low bow. "My apologies, Professor."

"Accepted. Now, young man, I must speak to Nick privately."

Harry grabbed his vodka and tonic. "Of course."

"By the way, Harry, where were you Sunday evening?"

"I assure you, Professor, I had something more satisfying to do with my time than shoot at Natalie," Harry replied, turning aft. "I'll leave it to Nick to explain."

Woolley looked at Nick quizzically.

Nick leaned close and whispered into Woolley's ear, "He claims he was making love to Sheila Stevens. No witnesses, however."

Woolley jerked away. "I should certainly hope not."

"You were looking for me. What's on your mind, my friend?"

Now Woolley whispered. "Not here."

Nick picked up his scotch. "Follow me. I know just the place."

When they entered the master suite, Woolley blurted, "Opulent in the extreme."

"Unless it belongs to you," said Nick. "Okay, what's so important?"

Woolley crossed the cabin to the window seat. "I've been doing what you asked of me," he said, sitting. "A bit of discreet eavesdropping."

Nick sat on the bed. "On whom?"

"Richard Edwards and that boy."

"Parker Slade?"

Woolley sipped his gin and tonic. "Yes. They were huddled by one of the stairs that go down to the fantail. I was seated alone, having my lunch. Edwards said, and this is an exact quote, 'Stop worrying, darling. I'll handle the Natalie problem. It will be settled for good tonight, and then we'll be off to Gay Paree.' "

"You interpreted that as meaning what?"

"Edwards intends to kill Natalie tonight and he and his lover plan a getaway to Paris. *Gay* Paree! What else could it mean?"

"Was that the entire conversation?"

"Unfortunately, Simon Cane chose that very moment to plop next to me and start jabbering about a federal case he's had to put on hold because of what he termed Natalie's nonsense. Edwards and Slade went into the lounge. I haven't seen them since."

Nick remembered Harry trying the door of the first cabin and finding it locked. "I have a pretty good idea where they went. What you overheard is worth thinking about. But don't be in quite such hurry to find me and report what you learn. We don't want to stir up suspicions among the passengers that we're something more than Natalie's weekend guests."

"I take your point."

"If asked to join a conversation, do so, but don't intrude and by no means do not try to direct it. Should anyone inquire as to why I've come along on this junket, stick to the cover story. I'm the entertainment Natalie promised."

"You can count on me, Nick."

"You return topside first. I'll follow in a few minutes."

When Woolley was gone, Nick left the master suite and listened for sounds in the cabin opposite. Hearing none, he tried the door and found it unlocked. Inside, he found a smaller version of the master suite unoccupied. The double bed had been disturbed and a half-hearted effort made to restore it. He also noted the lingering aroma of a strong cigar, probably Mexican, most likely a Te-Amo.

Fifteen

WOOLLEY CAME UP the spiral stairs and found lunch over and Ivo Bogdanovich lending Bill Restivo a hand in clearing the remnants of the buffet from the table. Restivo looked at Woolley with a solicitous smile. "May I get you something? Coffee? Tea? A liqueur?"

"No, thanks. My compliments on serving a wonderful lunch."

"It was my pleasure, sir."

"Will you also be arranging the meals after we arrive at our destination?"

"No, sir. Mrs. Goodman has a cook and maid. But I will be tending the bar."

"Very good. You mix a very nice drink. And what about you, Ivo? Does your boss have yet another sort of job in mind for you?"

"As you say, Mr. Woolley. She's the boss, so whatever she asks, I'll do."

"And very well, I'm sure."

Looking aft, he saw all the passengers gathered on the deck. Harry Hardin and Sheila Stevens were seated together on the couch at the rear. Looking seaward at the port rail, but in animated conversation, were Simon Cane and Nigel Wilson. On the starboard side, Clifford Branson was speaking to Richard Edwards, who clasped a tall drink in his left hand and had his right arm slung loosely around Parker Slade's waist.

As Woolley emerged from the dimly illuminated lounge, he squinted against bright sunlight and wondered if their division was purposeful or random. Mindful of Nick's admonitions, he made no effort to join any group until Edwards let go of Slade, strode across the deck, and declared, "Professor Woolley, your wardrobe is absolutely magnificent, perfect for the occasion. If I didn't know you're not an actor, I'd think you were an extra sent by Central Casting to dress up the set! I'm Rich Edwards, coproducer of *Smoking Out a Killer*. Please join us."

Taking Woolley by the arm, he led him to the others.

"Do you know Cliff Branson?"

Woolley affected a slight bow. "Only his reputation as a screenwriter."

Branson smiled wanly. "Good or bad?"

"And this young man is Parker Slade," said Edwards, gripping the youth's shoulder. "In my opinion, he's the new Leonardo DiCaprio, but with a much nicer build."

Slade's greeting was a nod of the head and "You're the guy who wrote the book?"

"That's right."

"It must be a pretty good book to get made into a movie."

"I'll be happy to send you a copy."

"That's okay. I read the script."

"Which character are you playing?"

"The one that killed the old man."

"That would be Rex Trevellyan. Are you happy about playing a killer in your first film?"

Slade glanced at Edwards. "Well, it's not really my first."

"Parker's had a couple of bit parts in a couple of small productions," said Edwards, "but this is going to be his breakout role."

Branson said, "You probably hear this from people all the time, Professor Woolley, but I've been giving some thought to trying my hand at writing a novel, and I was hoping that some time during this weekend you might listen to what I have in mind."

"I'd be delighted to do so."

"But no pulling punches. If you think I should forget about it and stick to movies, I want you to give it to me straight."

"You have my word."

"It's refreshing to hear that. In my present line of work when someone says that to me, I figure I'd better call my agent to get it in writing."

"What sort of novel are you thinking about? A bare-knuckle, no-holds-barred exposé of the Hollywood system?"

Branson's eyes shifted in the direction of the port side. "That's a very tempting subject." The eyes came back to Woolley. "But I'm thinking about a murder story. I've always been fascinated by the idea that someone feels such hatred toward another person that he chooses to murder." He flashed a nervous smile. "Not that I have any personal experience!"

"I believe it's a rare individual who hasn't contemplated murder, albeit fleetingly. It was, I think, the famed defense attorney Clarence Darrow who quipped, 'I have never killed a man, but I have read many obituaries with a lot of pleasure!' "

Branson laughed. "I like you, Woolley. I knew when I read your novel about Nick Chase that I would." His eyes shifted again as Nick emerged from the lounge. "Ah, here's that man himself. Right on cue! I've been dying to talk to him."

Woolley turned and beckoned to Nick.

"So, Mr. Chase," said Edwards, "are you working on a case at the moment?"

"Call me Nick. I'm just along for the ride." He took out his cigar case. "Do you gentlemen mind if I smoke?"

"Not at all," said Edwards, reaching for a packet of cigars in his shirt pocket. "I'll light one up with you."

Nick carefully removed a red-and-gold band and tucked it into a pocket.

"Ah," Edwards said, "I see you're a band off guy. What's your brand?"

Nick held up the cigar. "This is an H. Upmann1844."

"Very nice!"

"I see you prefer Te-Amos."

Edwards glanced at Parker Slade. "These were a present."

"There's a customer who comes to my store regularly," Nick said, trimming the end of the Upmann, "who says that the best cigar is the one someone gives you."

"What's your feeling about Cuban cigars? I think they're overrated and overpriced."

"Not to mention illegal in the U.S.," Nick said, turning his back to the wind to light up.

The yacht was cutting through placid, sun-dappled water within sight of the shore, having left behind the Massachusetts towns of Salem and Beverly, and making speed toward Gloucester with its famous statue of a fisherman and a three-day St. Peter's Fiesta and pontifical mass in June to bless the fishing fleet. Soon after, they would pass Cape Ann and lose sight of land until they reached the Isles of Shoals.

Finding no point in continuing to converse with the three men with Nick present to pick up any clues they might inadvertently drop, Woolley interjected, "If you fellows intend to discuss the virtues of one brand of cigar over another, this *pipe* smoker asks to be excused." With the aroma of wind-blown smoke from two cigars preceding him, he sauntered to the stern.

Sixteen

"WHAT'S THE MATTER with you?" Harry asked as he and Sheila made room for Woolley on the couch. "Not seasick, I hope?"

"I got my sea legs long ago. It's just that once you get Nick Chase going on the subject of stogies, there's no stopping him. You will discover this truth when he lectures us on the subject after dinner this evening—or tomorrow or Sunday, if that's Natalie's plan."

"I'm looking forward to it," Harry said, "although I'd much rather hear him on the topic of his murder cases."

"On that matter you'll find him quite reticent. I've been after him to sit down and write his memoirs. He adamantly refuses. He says there have already been way too many books by ex-cops. I would have preferred to write *Smoking Out a Killer* as a true crime book. I had to settle for the novel form."

"And you did a swell job of it! When Natalie sent me a copy, I couldn't put it down. My only request of Natalie when she asked me to play Rick Gordon was that I have a say in whom she picked to adapt it to the screen. I urged her to get Sheila, of course. But she went with Cliff Branson and lived to rue the day. He absolutely trashed your fine book by inserting gratuitous violence, nudity, and a car chase. Can you imagine it?"

Woolley chuckled. "Nick in the nude?"

"Well, the nude scene involves the young man, Rex Trevellyan, and the girl who works in the antique shop."

"I'd hardly call Sara Hobart a girl. She's twice Rex's age."

"Thanks to Sheila being brought onto the picture," said Harry, giving her a hug, "that's been fixed. But thanks to Rich Edwards, the audience is still going to get a look at Rex, that is to say Parker Slade, in the buff."

"Mr. Edwards expects the role of Rex to be Parker Slade's—what was the term he used? Breakthrough. Yes, a breakthrough role."

"Break*out* role," said Sheila.

Harry said, "Rich has been trying to sell that line to anyone he can find who'll listen."

"You have doubts?"

"The part of Rex is a very good one, and there have been guys who made a successful transition from beefcake to actor—Arnold Schwarzenegger, for instance, and Marky Mark who went from Calvin Klein underwear ads to Mark Wahlberg—but I'm not aware of any who made it from the hard-core porno film industry, even with a change of name and hair color."

Woolley's eyes went wide. "Parker Slade made dirty movies?"

"Videos, actually," said Sheila.

"Both kinds," Harry added.

Woolley shook his head. "Both kinds?"

"Straight and gay."

Woolley sighed. "My word."

"That's how Rich discovered him," said Harry. "He was at a party in West Hollywood and saw one of the videos. A gay one, of course. It was apparently love at first sight. I've heard that Rich threw out a veritable dragnet in the porn industry to find him. I also have it from a very reliable source who saw Parker's videotaped audition that Rich, shall we say, *directed* it."

Woolley's eyes widened farther. "By *directed it*, you mean—?"

Harry smiled slyly. "Do you think the casting couch is a Hollywood myth?"

"Does Natalie know about this?"

"If she doesn't," said Sheila, "she's the only one on the picture."

"Perhaps she does know but doesn't care."

"I suppose that is possible," said Harry.

Woolley looked forward at Slade. "He is certainly handsome. The real Rex Trevellyan was a very good-looking young man."

"Good-looking young men are available at a dime a dozen in Hollywood," said Harry. "Perhaps Parker Slade is also a good actor."

"It wouldn't be the first time that a young man or woman rose from a casting couch," said Sheila, "and became a movie star whose name goes above the title."

"I personally hope Parker can pull it off," Harry said, "and if there's anything I can do to help it happen, I will."

"That's most commendable of you, Harry," said Woolley.

"As long as he knows his lines, hits his mark, avoids bumping into the furniture, and doesn't get in the way of my light."

The aroma of cigar smoke swayed Woolley's attention to Nick, still talking with Edwards, while Cliff Branson stood braced against the starboard rail, as still as a statue and probably bored. Perched on the top, arms resting on parted thighs, long hands dangling between them, and feet hooked around the lower rung, blond hair being tossed by the wind, Parker Slade resembled a seabird with a yellow crest.

Gazing at him and mindful of all that Harry and Sheila had conveyed about Slade and his relationship with Edwards, he recalled Rich's words to Slade.

Stop worrying, darling.

Stop worrying about what? Slade's past? The videotaped audition? Was that the Natalie problem? Might she not have known what everyone else apparently knew, until now? Was that what was to be settled for good tonight?

Certainly, this was important, Woolley thought, but Nick had told him not to be in a hurry to report what he'd learned, lest suspicions be aroused among the passengers that they were not merely Natalie's guests, but detectives.

Looking forward, he saw that the conversation that had been going on for some time at the port rail between Nigel Wilson and Simon Cane ended with the former turning abruptly and going into the lounge, leaving the latter with an expression that appeared to be highly agitated.

Neither did this escape the attention of Harry Hardin. "There seems to have been a clash of the titans. I wonder who won, the legal eagle or the barracuda?"

Cane left the rail and turned toward them. He arrived looking composed.

"Could anyone ask for a more splendid day for a cruise? It's good to see you, Sheila."

"Hello, Simon."

"And how are you, Harry?"

"Just fine. Have you met our esteemed author, Roger Woolley?"

"It's a pleasure I've long anticipated."

Woolley stood and they shook hands.

"I feel I know you through your books," said Cane. "They are marvelous reads. I've been a devotee of mysteries since my college days. I suppose by now I should be able to figure out who done it, but I never can. The clues seem to go right by me. I admire your skill in planting them so cleverly in your novels."

"When you start out knowing who done it, it's not hard to do. The main thing is to play fair and put the reader on the same footing as the sleuth. No surprises on the last page."

"Wouldn't it be wonderful if life were like that?"

"If it were, Simon," said Harry, "there would be no need for contracts and lawyers."

"On the other hand, if life were fair and people were always on the up and up, there'd be nothing on which to base plots for movies. And without movies, how would you make a living?"

"Happily for both of us, Simon, we're both guaranteed comfortable incomes."

"I wonder if I might take Mr. Woolley away from you?"

"There's no need," Harry said, getting to his feet and extending a hand to Sheila. "We were about to go inside for a cool drink."

"Such a surprising couple," said Cane, sitting beside Woolley as Harry and Sheila entered the lounge.

Woolley dug in a pocket for a pipe and tobacco. "Surprising?"

"Completely mismatched. Wrong for each other."

"I wouldn't know."

"Of course you wouldn't, but they are."

Packing the pipe, Woolley asked, "Is the relationship between Harry and Sheila what you wished to talk to me about?"

"Actually, I'm more interested in your relationship with Harry."

"Oh? What about it?"

"It's obvious that he regards you very highly. He's a great admirer of your novels."

"What is your point?"

Cane smiled. "Natalie told me you were not a man to put up with someone beating around the bush. Very well, I'll get to my point. I'm worried that if a situation arises concerning Sheila's role in the making of this movie, Harry might do something rash. My hope is that you would undertake to persuade him that it would not be in anyone's interest for him to do anything precipitate, especially not in his interest."

"If this is getting to your point, Mr. Cane, you are not succeeding. Out with it, please."

Cane looked around anxiously. "I tell you this in confidence."

"Yes, yes, man, of course."

"Natalie is intent upon firing Sheila as screenwriter."

"How would that affect Harry?"

"I'm afraid that if she does so, Harry will quit. Without

Harry Hardin, this film will be doomed. Production will cease."

"Doesn't he have a contract?"

"Of course, but you know as well as I that a contract is only as good as the will of the parties who sign it."

"Which you of all people should know is why we have courts of law."

"The strength of our legal system lies not in resolving issues at the bar, but in settling them before they get to court."

"If you are Natalie's lawyer, why are you turning to me to persuade Harry not to violate his contract? You should take up this matter with Harry Hardin's attorney."

"But there's the rub. I *am* Harry's attorney."

"Good lord, man," Woolley exclaimed, poking the pipe into Cane's chest. "Where are your ethics?"

"This was a straightforward deal, good for both Natalie and Harry. Until now."

Woolley angrily pocketed the pipe. "And a good deal for you, too, no doubt."

"The point is, there will be no problem if Harry acquiesces in Natalie's decision to fire Sheila as writer, if in fact that is what Natalie has in mind."

"It seems to me the solution to this situation is for Natalie to keep Sheila as writer."

"You've known Natalie longer than anyone involved in the picture. Have you ever known her to compromise on principle?"

"How is principle at stake in this? It's a business decision. If firing Sheila means Harry walking off the picture, don't fire her. If Natalie is unhappy with the script, as apparently she is, she should bring in someone else to collaborate with her."

"Sheila wouldn't stand for it. But she is not the problem. It's Harry and what he might do if Sheila is replaced. That is why I hoped you would agree to help everyone out of this mess by showing Harry that nothing is to be gained by him quitting. If he walks off the picture, it will be a disaster for all the people working on this film. And it will destroy

New Millennium Films. You can prevent that calamity by talking sense to Harry."

"The sensible thing would be for Sheila to resign as screenwriter."

"The effect on Harry would be the same," said Cane, gazing at the sea. "He's madly in love with Sheila. Have you ever been in love, Mr. Woolley?"

"Not enough to throw away a multi-million-dollar contract. Perhaps the proper course for me is to have a chat with Natalie in hope of persuading her to reconsider dismissing Sheila."

"Your chances of achieving that goal are as likely as persuading Natalie to hand over the reins of New Millennium to Richard Edwards. If Rich were running the show, there would be no problem with keeping Sheila on the picture. But as long as Natalie's in the catbird seat, the only hope of avoiding disaster is to keep Harry Hardin from walking. I believe you're the only person who can accomplish that."

"You overestimate my influence."

"Will you please try, sir?"

"How certain are you that Natalie is determined to fire Sheila?"

"If I weren't, I wouldn't be bothering you."

"You put me in an awkward position."

Cane stood and looked down at Woolley. "I know. I wish it weren't necessary."

As he walked away, Woolley retrieved the pipe from the pocket, lit it, and muttered, "Very awkward."

A shadow fell across his face.

"What's the matter my friend?" asked Nick, bending over him "A touch of *mal de mer*?"

Woolley looked up. "I am not seasick," he said sharply. "Why does everyone keep asking me if I'm seasick?"

"Probably because you look like you are."

"Well, I'm not. So back off!"

Nick held up his hands defensively. "Okay, okay."

"I have a great deal to tell you," Woolley said, looking around the deck, "but I must be sure we're not overheard.

I suggest we retire to the cabin we used before."

"That's too obvious. How about the flybridge? Up there we'll look like a couple of landlubbers enjoying the view."

Reached by a ladder on the port side, the topmost deck had a windscreen at the forward end and a control console that was a duplicate of the one below. An aft sitting area in the form of a couch that accommodated three was tucked beneath a superstructure supporting the ship's revolving radar antenna. With wind tossing his gray hair, Nick smiled at Woolley. "Now, what have you learned that's obviously upset you?"

He listened intently, arms folded across his chest, as Woolley recounted his conversation with Harry and Sheila and the awkward request made by Simon Cane.

When Woolley finished his narratives, Nick thought a moment and said, "The inference to be drawn from what you've been told about the relationship between Edwards and Slade and the matter of the video that Edwards made with the kid, is that Natalie somehow got hold of the tape and that Edwards intends to get it back tonight. Have I got it right?"

"I believe Edwards is prepared to settle the matter by murdering her, if he must."

"That must be some tape! Did Harry and Sheila say they actually saw it?"

"If they know what's on it, they must have."

"Why should Natalie be concerned by the fact that Rich Edwards made a pornographic tape with Parker Slade?"

"If it were to become known—"

"Harry and Sheila know about it. Who's to say others don't also know?"

"I mean, if the public were to find out."

"From what I read in the papers and magazines about the present state of movie making and the taste of moviegoers, I'd guess that people would flock to the box office."

"Dismiss this information if you wish, Nick, but there's no dodging the fact that Edwards and Slade are up to no good. Bear in mind that if anything were to happen to Natalie, the one who takes over the production of the film is Rich Edwards."

"Murder seems an extreme way to do so. You assume that if Natalie is out of the way, Edwards gets control of New Millennium Films?"

"We have that on no less an authority than Simon Cane."

"According to Natalie, there are three other investors, who might feel they have something to say about who takes over. And don't forget Tony Biciano."

"According to Simon Cane, none of that will matter if Harry Hardin quits the film."

"Are you going to do what Cane asked and talk to Hardin?"

"Do I have any other option?"

"You could choose to heed the advice of a former movie actress by the name of Nancy Reagan and just say no."

"Joke all you wish," said Woolley, puffing on his pipe, "but I can't allow the production of the film to come to a screeching halt because of me."

"Do you truly believe that Harry Hardin is going to walk away from this movie, get sued, and probably risk not being cast in another movie because Natalie fired his girlfriend?"

"Simon Cane believes it's possible."

"By the way, in your conversation with him did he bring up the subject of the shots that were fired at Natalie last Sunday night?"

"He did not. But he couldn't have done it. He lives in New York."

"An hour's flight. A phone call away, if he has an accomplice."

"You've eliminated no one as a suspect?"

"Each of our companions on the good ship *Murder Two* appears to have a motive to kill Natalie. There are two guys who made a potentially embarrassing video, a lawyer on the horns of a conflict of interest brought on by a lapse of ethics, a couple of ambitious writers, a jilted lover with dreams of being a movie mogul, and a temperamental love-sick superstar."

PART V

Pirate's Cove

Seventeen

AT FIVE O'CLOCK Nick and Woolley entered the cockpit. "We must be getting pretty close to Pirate's Cove by now, Dave," said Nick.

"Just peeking above the horizon is the Shoals light," Kolker replied, pointing ahead.

The spot eluded Nick's searching gaze.

"Yes, yes, I see it," exclaimed Woolley. "It's barely a speck."

"It's on White Island. The first lighthouse station was built there in the late 1700s. This one was erected in 1859 and automated in 1987. It's now powered by solar energy."

Nick found the speck. "How far from White Island to Pirate's Cove?"

Kolker punched up a navigational chart on a video screen in the control console. "These nine large islands," he said, tracing a wide circle with a finger, "are known as the Isles of Shoals. The name comes from the shoals of fish in the area. These have always been very rich fishing grounds. The others are Appledore, which is the biggest, Star, Malaga, Cedar, Lunging, Duck, which is a wildlife refuge, and Smutty Nose. Duck is the farthest north and White is the farthest south. Next to it is Seavey's, named for an early inhabitant. It's said that he discovered some gold doubloons buried by the pirate Blackbeard. These islands were apparently one of the old seadog's favorite places for stashing loot. He also got married in these islands. One of his treasure burials is supposed to have been on Pirate's Cove."

Woolley bent close to the screen. "Which of these islands is it?"

Dave pointed to a triangular shape about eight miles due east of White. "Technically, Pirate's Cove is not considered one of the Isles of Shoals. In addition to the Blackbeard connection it's got an interesting history. During the First World War it was a navy radio station and in the Second World War it was used as a communications and radar base for supply convoys and troop ships heading across the North Atlantic. During the Cold War it was an army Nike missile base. The slip where we'll dock was built by the navy in 1940. When the island was declared surplus by the government about eight years ago, Mr. Goodman bought it. He used it as a base for deep-sea fishing. When he died, Mrs. Goodman built the house. She constructed it around some of the old navy and Nike buildings."

Woolley asked, "Which of these shapes is Smutty Nose?"

Kolker tapped a fingertip on a long island running east-west at the center of the group. "The name comes from black rocks on the eastern end that give it a smutchy appearance. That got twisted into Smutty Nose. It's the most famous of the Isles on account of a murder that was committed there over a hundred years ago."

"Longer ago than that," said Woolley enthusiastically. "It was in March of 1839, and there were two murders committed on Smutty Nose—with an axe. I hope to visit the island sometime this weekend. Perhaps you could take me over there, Dave."

"I'm sorry, Mr. Woolley, I can't. As soon as I leave you folks off at Pirate's Cove, I've got orders to take *Murder Two* into Portsmouth."

"Is there another way for me to get from Pirate's Cove to Smutty Nose?"

"There's bound to be someone in Portsmouth with a charter boat who'd be glad to come out and pick you up.

I can ask around if you wish and give you a call if I find anyone."

"Please do."

"It won't be cheap."

"Hang the cost. I'd hate to be this close to Smutty Nose and not visit the scene of the second most famous axe murder in New England. The first is the Lizzie Borden case."

"When was that?"

"In 1892. Surely, you've heard the poem:

> *Lizzie Borden took an axe*
> *And gave her mother forty whacks;*
> *And when she saw what she had done,*
> *She gave her father forty-one!"*

"Lizzie offed her parents, huh?"

"She was tried in Fall River, Massachusetts, for killing her father and *step*mother with twenty-nine, not eighty-one blows, and not with an axe, but a hatchet. She was found not guilty."

"Do you think she did it?"

"Yes. She got off because of shoddy police work and sympathetic public opinion."

"Are you an expert on murders?"

Nick answered, "Professor Woolley makes his living by committing at least one a year. But only within the pages of a book. He's a mystery writer."

"What's the cleverest way you ever had someone murdered?"

Woolley gave Nick a smile. "A poisoned cigar."

"Really? How did he get the victim to smoke it?"

"*She* gave him a box of his favorites, all poisoned, on his sixty-fifth birthday."

"That's some nasty old broad."

"Nasty, yes. A broad? In every respect. But a mere thirty-three years of age."

"I guess she bumped off the geezer for the good old motive of getting his money."

"Melissa's motive for murdering Michael was even older

than that. It was the green-eyed demon, jealousy. She objected to sharing him with a twenty-year-old mistress."

"The dirty old dog!"

Nick said, "Dave, I hope that many years from now you experience the thrill of discovering that it is possible to be sixty-five years old and not be considered a *geezer*."

"Sorry, sir. No offense intended."

Smiling, Nick gave the young man a tap on the shoulder. "And that you can romance a younger woman without being regarded as a dirty old dog." Leaving the cockpit, he turned and added, "Or being murdered for it."

Presently, *Murder Two* arrived in sight of Pirate's Cove.

As she skirted the island on the south, the passengers clustered on the aft deck and along the port rail. Nick and Woolley were on the bow.

About a mile away, the island slanted at a steep angle for what Nick estimated was a mile from a high ridge of black rock on the western end to a plateau on the east that seemed to be a shelf supported by cliffs jutting from the dark and brooding ocean.

"Dreary-looking spot," Woolley said. "It must be wicked here in a hurricane."

At the moment, except for a couple of seagulls riding an updraft, the pale-blue sky was featureless, the wind light from the south, and the greenish-black water calm, save for low waves that turned foamy white as they lapped the feet of the sheer, slate-gray cliffs. These were topped by a blanket of low shrubs and a scattering of wind-tortured trees. There was no sign of a house.

It came into view as Dave Kolker maneuvered *Murder Two* toward the eastern tip of the island. Appearing to hug the ground, the house was low and rambling with gray, fortresslike walls, a few small, round windows, and a flat roof whose line was broken by four low-rising stone chimneys. "Very disappointing," said Woolley.

"What did you expect?" Nick asked.

Woolley puffed a cloud of aromatic smoke from his pipe. "Baskerville Hall, of course."

*   *   *

As the yacht rounded a point, Natalie Goodman adjusted the focus of the binoculars and scanned it from bow to stern. "Everyone's on board."

"Really, Natalie," said Tony Biciano, "did you think any of them wouldn't be?"

"The way Simon Cane was carrying on about having to prepare for a case that goes to trial on Monday," she said, handing him the binoculars, "I thought he might decide not to come."

"Fat chance," Tony said, finding the lawyer at the stern. "That shyster knows exactly what side his bread is buttered on."

Natalie reclaimed the binoculars. "It's time for you to get your clothes on and head down to the dock. On your way, tell Nora and the maid you hired for the weekend—what's her name?"

"Felicity Dane."

"Tell her and Nora that there will indeed be nine guests for dinner and that I want everything ready by eight o'clock. And please send the bartender to me as soon as possible."

On *Murder Two* the passengers were astir, preparing to land.

Looking at the island from amidships on the port side, Rich Edwards had an arm around Parker Slade's slender waist. "I'm not sure whether this is going to be a weekend in paradise," he said languidly, "or three nights and two days on Devil's Island. It's entirely up to Natalie."

Slade flipped a cigarette into the water. "Screw her. She doesn't run the world."

"Watch what you say, my dear. Loose lips can sink not only ships, but incipient careers," Edwards said, tightening his hold and looking sidelong at Nigel Wilson and Simon Cane a few feet away. The latter leaned against the rail with a cell phone pressed to his left ear.

*   *   *

The phone had proved useless.

"We're out of range," Cane said, pocketing it.

Nigel Wilson shrugged. "So much for technology."

The only way to find out how the pretrial meeting had gone, Cane thought, was either by using the ship-to-shore radio or waiting to use a telephone in Natalie's house. Peering at it across the water, he said, "I don't mind telling you, Nigel, I think that it's a monstrosity. It's almost impossible to get to, and once you do, it's a most inhospitable and uncomfortable dwelling."

"Don't I know it," said Wilson bitterly.

"Yes, you were here in happier times. Perhaps they will return."

"Natalie and I are strictly business partners."

Uncertain what to say and unable to go on looking at the house, Cane gazed astern and found Harry Hardin and Sheila Stevens, a pair of lovebirds cuddling on the couch.

Aware that Cane was watching, Harry turned to Sheila and kissed her. When he drew back, she gasped, "What in hell prompted that?"

Harry feigned shock. "You didn't enjoy it?"

"Sure, I did, but—"

"Simon Cane was looking this way," Harry said with a giggle. "I thought it would be fun to show him our solidarity."

Circling him with her arms and tilting back her head, she said, "Show him again."

"Too late. He's not looking anymore."

"Kiss me again anyway."

"You really are wicked. I wouldn't be surprised if it was you who shot at Natalie."

"I think you were very gallant in telling Nick that we were making love at the time."

"Did you try to kill Natalie?"

"If I did, my darling," she whispered as she brushed his lips with hers, "by lying to Nick you've made yourself an accomplice after the fact."

*   *   *

Having joined Nick and Woolley at the bow, Cliff Branson intoned:

> *"And down in fathoms many went the captain and*
> *the crew;*
> *Down went the owners—greedy men whom hope*
> *of gain allured:*
> *Oh, dry the starting tear, for they were heavily*
> *insured."*

Woolley barked a laugh. " 'Etiquette.' Correct?"

"You certainly know your W. S. Gilbert!"

" 'And I'm never, never sick at sea!' "

" 'What never?' "

" 'No, never!' "

" 'What, *never?*' "

" 'Hardly ever!' "

" 'He's hardly ever sick at sea.' "

" 'Then give three cheers, and one cheer more.' "

" 'For the hardy Captain of the *Pinafore!*' " Woolley roared a laugh. "I played the captain in a college production."

"And I was once the handsome sailor," said Branson. "What about you, Nick? Did you ever take to the stage?"

"Thankfully, no," said Nick, taking the cigar from his mouth, "but if it's poetry you want, try this:

> *"Twas off the blue Canary isles,*
> *A glorious summer day,*
> *I sat upon the quarter deck,*
> *And whiffed my cares away;*
> *And as the volumed smoke arose,*
> *Like incense in the air,*
> *I breathed a sigh to think, in sooth,*
> *It was my last cigar."*

Eighteen

WHEN *MURDER TWO* rounded a rocky point on the eastern tip of Pirate's Cove Island and sailed into an inlet that seemed to have been gouged out of the land by a giant ice-cream scoop, the passengers were afforded a dramatically different view of Natalie Goodman's house. With an eastern facade of glass and wood overlooking a wide, low-walled terrace, it sat atop a hill that shelved gently to the water in a broad sweep of lush lawn and flowerbeds. From one of these rose a tall flagpole flying the Stars and Stripes. Below it flapped a triangular blue pennant with the letters N, M, and F intertwined in gold, the logo of New Millennium Films.

"Now, this is what I'd hoped for," Woolley said to Nick.

"I thought you wanted Baskerville Hall."

Standing next to Woolley, Sheila Stevens said, "If you think this layout is grand, you should see Natalie's place in the Santa Barbara mountains. She calls it her ranch. Some ranch! I have yet to see a horse or a cow."

"If you ever did, my dear," said Harry Hardin, "you'd be scared out of your wits."

At the foot of a wide flagstone stairway that curved down gracefully from Natalie's house to the dock, Tony Biciano waited in a white short-sleeve shirt with a pale-blue scarf,

knee-length crisp white shorts, high white socks, and canvas deck shoes. With hands jammed in the pockets of the
shorts, he looked like a model showing the latest fashion
in yachting gear.

As he watched, *Murder Two* responded to Dave Kolker's
masterful handling and touched the wharf portside with a
gentle kiss.

Over the yacht's public address system, Kolker said,
"Folks, please remain on board until we're tied up."

With that, Ivo Bogdanovich bounded from the bow with
a rope in hand, looped it around a stanchion with the skill
of an old salt, and dashed aft to tie up the stern.

Kolker cut the engines. "Welcome to Pirate's Cove. I
hope you've enjoyed the voyage and wish you a pleasant
weekend. I'll see you all again Monday morning."

"Assuming, that is," muttered Sheila, "that we all survive."

Ivo said to the passengers, "Just leave your luggage on
the boat. I'll bring it up."

He had pressed Bill Restivo into service to help him
bring luggage up from the crew quarters. "Imagine what it
must be like to do this job on a big ocean liner like the
QE2," said Ivo, lugging Nigel Wilson's heavy bag up the
ladder. "Have you ever been on a cruise ship, Bill?"

"Only once."

"As a guest? Or was it a job?"

He'd been given two tickets to Aruba, part of the payment for a party he'd catered for a Wall Street executive,
who had insisted that all the waiters be handsome and do
the serving bare-chested. The occasion was a Fourth of July
party. Rich Edwards had been there. That had eventually
led to this weekend's party. He'd accepted only because of
the promise of a part in the movie.

"I was on vacation," he said in answer to Ivo's question.
"This is the first time I've been bartender on a yacht."

"Some day I'm gonna own one of these myself," said
Ivo, "but on the West Coast. I'll be a movie producer then,

and the crew will be gorgeous babes looking to break into films."

"Why a producer? You're good-looking enough to be in the movies yourself."

"Natalie Goodman told me the way to survive in Hollywood isn't acting in movies," said Ivo, placing Nigel Wilson's bag on the deck, "it's being in a position to *hire* the actors."

As the passengers stepped from deck to dock, Tony Biciano met each with a smile and alternate "Hi, there, welcome to the island," "Glad to see you," "I hope you had a good trip," and "Natalie will see you all for cocktails." When everyone was off the yacht, he said, "Just to make everything easier for you in case you need something, Natalie's hired a maid and sort of all-round assistant. Her name is Felicity. The cook's name is Nora. Just as he did on the boat, Bill Restivo will handle the bar. Cocktails will be served at six in the main parlor. Dinner's at seven."

Waiting in a large, airy foyer to guide the guests to rooms were the cook and maid. Nora was middle-aged with black hair tied back in a knot, short, stout, and reserved behind a white apron. Felicity appeared to be in her twenties with short blond hair crowned by a white cap, a black dress with a high collar, and a small white-lace apron.

"I hope you won't think I'm forward," Woolley said to Felicity as she escorted him and Nick to their bedrooms on the south side of the house, "but I think you're pretty enough to be in movies." He turned to Nick. "Don't you agree, Nick?"

"Absolutely!"

"Thank you, gentlemen," she said, "but I don't think I'm cut out to be an actress. I had a part in a play in high school, and I was just awful. I really want to go into hotel services. I'm taking courses. I'd like to be a hotel manager someday or maybe a cruise director."

"So you're getting a head start by working as a maid in the meantime," said Nick.

"Just for the summer. I'm registered with a service in

Portsmouth. What I earn will go toward the tuition. It does cost quite a bit of money."

Woolley exclaimed, "Everything worthwhile does, my dear."

When she was out of hearing, Nick poked a finger in Woolley's ribs. "I'm surprised at you, Professor. A man your age, flirting with a housemaid!"

"I was not flirting. I merely observed, rightly, that she is a very attractive girl—and a lot more attractive than some of the women I see in movies and on television these days."

At that moment, Ivo appeared with their bags. "Excuse me, Nick," he said, "but once you and Mr. Woolley are settled in, Natalie would like to see you. I'm to wait around and show you the way."

"No time like the present, Ivo."

"Very good. I'll just put your bags in your rooms and we'll be off."

He led them through a maze of corridors with closed doors.

"Her room's on the other side of the house," Ivo said. "This place is so big and has so many rooms and hallways you could easily get lost."

"You seem to know your way around," said Woolley.

"Preproduction meetings were held here. We were having them on the West Coast, but one day Natalie came back from her ranch and sent a memo to everyone announcing she was shifting the meetings to here."

Nick asked, "Did she explain why?"

"Natalie never explains."

"The shift must have caused a lot of disruption."

"I'll say it did," Ivo replied, stopping before a large white door. "This is it. Do you think you can find your way back?"

"If not," Nick said, "we'll send up flares."

"That's a good one," said Ivo, knocking on the door.

Natalie opened it. "Hello, Nick. Professor. That's all for now, Ivo. Come in, gentlemen."

The room was an enormous office. Six maroon leather armchairs formed a semicircle in front of a large desk, which faced south. Floor-to-ceiling windows afforded an ocean panorama.

Woolley exclaimed, "What a spectacular view!"

"For what it cost me," Natalie said, sitting at the desk, "it better be spectacular."

"How many rooms do you have?"

"In this suite there are three. This office, a parlor, and a very large bedroom. The house has ten rooms on this floor—not counting the living room, dining room, and kitchen. There are another six in the basement and a small screening room."

"You'd never know it by seeing the house from the water," said Woolley

"How was the trip from Boston?"

"As smooth as silk," said Nick as he and Woolley sat in side-by-side chairs.

"*Murder Two* is quite a comfortable vessel," said Woolley.

"I wasn't asking about the accommodations. Did you pick up any clues regarding which of the passengers has been trying to murder me?"

Nick replied, "Nothing conclusive."

"Whom do you suspect?"

"Excuse the cliché, Natalie, but at the moment I suspect everyone. It appears that each of the people you've brought up here for this weekend could have a motive."

"If they didn't, I wouldn't have invited them."

"The memo you sent them was hardly a friendly invitation."

"Who showed it to you?"

"I believe it was Sheila's that I saw. By the way, she and Harry Hardin have an alibi for the night that shots were fired at you. They insist that at the time they were making love in their room."

"She lies and he backs her up."

"Why not, *he* lies and *she* backs *him* up?"

"Because Harry has no reason to murder me."

"Then why did you invite him here?"

"I had to invite Harry to ensure that Sheila would come.

In that relationship, you must take one to get the other."

"Explain again why you think Sheila might want to see you dead."

"To avoid being fired from the film."

"It's my understanding that she gets paid regardless."

"Yes, but if I fire her, she won't get the screen credit."

"Do you intend to dismiss her?"

"Yes. It's an appalling script."

"If that's so, why didn't you fire Sheila when you first read it?"

"I'd hoped for improvements in the rewriting."

"I admit I don't know anything about the movie business, but wasn't there another reason why you kept Sheila Stevens on the picture for so long?"

"I don't know what you're getting at."

"You said it yourself. Because of the relationship between Harry and Sheila, to get the one you have to take the other. I think it was Harry that you wanted, but you knew that to get him you had to take Sheila on as screenwriter. Now that you've succeeded in getting Harry on board, you have no further need for Sheila. Because Harry's locked in by contract, you are free to give Sheila her walking papers."

"I believe you've made my point, Nick. With Harry committed by contract to making the picture, Sheila has no leverage to force me to keep her as writer. But with me out of the way, she stays on."

"How could she be sure of that?"

"Rich Edwards would take over. He'd keep her on."

"But Sheila has no guarantee of that."

"She thinks she has leverage with him. She expects to have Rich by the short hairs. And I mean that literally!"

"Are you referring to a certain videotape that's, shall we say, of a compromising nature?"

"You are very, very good, Nick. How did you learn about it?"

Nick smiled. "How did you find out about it?"

"Someone sent it to me. Anonymously. Someone wanted to discredit Richard."

"Have you any idea who would want to do that?"

"Practically everyone who accompanied you from Boston on *Murder Two,* with the exception of Rich's lover, of course, young Parker Slade."

"And Sheila Stevens."

"I see your point. If Sheila were trying to murder me so that Rich Edwards will take over as the producer of the film, she has no reason to send me the tape. The last thing she'd want is for me to fire Rich by invoking the morality cause in his contract. She's counting on him taking over when I'm dead."

"If both you and Edwards were out of the picture—no joke intended—who would replace you in charge of the production?"

"That decision would fall into the hands of the board of directors, but I expect that they would go along with whatever Nigel Wilson wants."

"Might Nigel propose that the picture be abandoned?"

"Not on your tintype. Nigel would kill to become head of a studio. That's why I put him on the guest list for this weekend."

"Is that Nigel's only reason to want to kill you?"

"If you are alluding to our previous romantic relationship, I assure you that Nigel is a man who would never be so silly as to kill for love. For money? Yes. For power? In a New York minute. Or should I say a Hollywood minute?"

"Why is Simon Cane here?"

"In addition to being my attorney, Simon is the executor of my estate. If I die, Simon becomes an even richer man."

"Two of the attempts that were made on your life were on the West Coast. Was Cane in California at the time?"

"On both occasions there was a preproduction meeting, and Simon attended. He flew out to L.A. in my plane with Nigel Wilson and Rich Edwards. They'd been back East raising money. All the others on the list live in California."

"Have they all been to your ranch in Santa Barbara?"

"Each year I put on a rodeo for charity. Everyone who is anyone in Hollywood comes."

"Why do you regard Clifford Branson as a suspect?"

"I did fire him."

"But you're planning to rehire him."

"At the time I sent the invitations to this weekend I hadn't made that decision. In retrospect, I shouldn't have included him on the suspect list. However, I'm glad I did, because Cliff is a most amusing guy to have at a party. You have my permission to disregard him as a suspect. That leaves how many?"

"If you are also excluding Harry Hardin and Parker Slade, it's four."

"I can't see Harry and Parker as suspects, but one of them could be an accomplice. Now, if there's nothing else, I should see about getting ready to play the gracious hostess. By the way, if you're not averse to getting out of bed early, Tony is organizing a fishing excursion tomorrow. The boat shoves off at six o'clock"

Woolley said, "I may take you up on that, Natalie."

"The only fish I'm interested in," Nick said, "is the one I find on a dinner plate."

Nineteen

WHILE SHEILA STEVENS sat combing her hair before a large antique mirror above a dressing table of dubious provenance, Harry Hardin stood close to the wall opposite a double bed covered with a thick quilt embroidered with whales. Studying a framed map of the island dated 1655, he noted that approximately where Natalie's house now stood the map was inscribed with a large X and the crudely printed word TREASURE.

"Sheel, do you suppose this thing is genuine?"

"I've always assumed Natalie had it made by the studio art department."

Harry sank to the bed, eyes still on the map. "I wonder if pirates really buried treasure."

"Only in the imaginations of Robert Louis Stevenson and Cecil B. DeMille."

"I think it would be fun to make a pirate movie. When this business with Natalie is behind us, how'd you like to write one for me?"

"What I know about pirates wouldn't fill a page."

"How much did you know about the stocks and bonds racket before you wrote *A Killing on Wall Street?*" He smiled. "Or murder, for that matter?"

"Everything I needed to know for that script I learned over one dinner at 21 with Nigel Wilson. We were seated at the same table that Burt Lancaster and Tony Curtis used in *Sweet Smell of Success.*"

"That's the second time on this picture that movie's been brought up to me," Harry said, getting off the bed. "On the first day of shooting Nick Chase told me that he was a cop keeping pain-in-the-ass onlookers off West Fifty-second Street when they were shooting that film. Nice guy, Nick. I wonder what he's doing here."

Sheila finished combing. "The motion picture you're starring in *is* based on a book that's based on him."

Harry continued studying the map. "Yeah, but that's not the reason Natalie's dragged him up to her island getaway. Shall I tell you why?"

Sheila turned her attention to earrings. "Pray do, darling."

Harry turned away from the map and looked at Sheila's reflection. "I believe Natalie's hired Nick to find out who's been trying to kill her."

"Don't be silly. If Natalie wanted a private detective, she would not have turned to a man who's been retired from the police for ages and now runs a cigar store."

"None of that stood in the way of Nick solving the murder case in our movie. Who better for Natalie to hire than Nick Chase? Anyone else she brought in would stick out like the proverbial sore thumb. Nick is perfect casting. Who do you think he suspects?"

"If you're so sure he's working as Natalie's detective," Sheila said, opting for plain gold loops, "why don't you ask him?"

"Darling, that might work in a scene in a movie, but this is a real-life drama that we are involved in, so I think I'll skip the theatrics, observe how detective Nick Chase plays his part, and react accordingly."

The decoration on the wall of Simon Cane's north-facing room was a large black-and-white photograph of an up-raised Nike missile surrounded by young men wearing helmets and army fatigue uniforms. A Cold War moment of readiness off the coast of New England. Hard to believe,

now that the Soviet Union was a shambles, that such dili-
gence had been necessary. Even harder to believe, he
thought, as picked up the bedside telephone to call New
York, that the downfall of Communism had been precipi-
tated by a former movie actor named Ronald Reagan.

Looking around the room and out the window to the
ocean, he waited with mounting impatience for someone in
his offices to answer. So what if it was well past five on a
Friday afternoon? Someone ought to be there.

On the sixth ring a junior associate, Jonathan Wilde, answered, "Law offices of Simon Cane. How may I help
you?"

"It's me. Where's Leiberman?"

"He just left, sir. I might be able to catch him at the
elevator."

"No, no. I'll try him at home tonight."

"Mr. Leiberman did try to reach you on your cell phone
several times today."

"The damn boat I was on was way out of range. Any
messages for me?"

"The only call slip with your name on it, sir, is from nine
o'clock this morning from a Mr. Biciano. There's no message. Just a note that he called."

"Thank you, Wilde. I plan to be back in town as early
as possible on Monday."

"Very good, sir. Have a pleasant weekend."

Cane hung up the phone thinking a pleasant weekend
was not bloody likely. And what a typical device of Natalie's to have Biciano phone the office to check on him,
to see if he was on his way to Boston. Yet it was peculiar,
he thought, as he got off the bed to change clothes for
cocktails and dinner, that Tony had given his name.

In the bedroom next to Cane's, occupied by Nigel Wilson, the motif of two walls was the sea. Four large water-
colors depicted two fishermen hauling in a catch, a
schooner under full sail, the Shoals lighthouse, and the
Spanish ship *Sagunto*, which had been driven aground on
Smutty Nose by a raging snowstorm on January 14, 1813,

at the cost of fourteen Spaniards, whom Samuel Haley found washed ashore and dead in snowdrifts the next morning.

Of all the bedrooms in Natalie's house, this was Nigel's favorite because it had been the one in which he'd first made love to her. But to his lasting and bitter regret it was also the last.

By the next summer she had discovered handsome, black-haired, smoldering-eyed, olive-skinned, and muscular Tony Biciano. A1990s Sal Mineo, but, to Natalie's relief and eventual delight, sexually straight, he had been waiting on tables in a Sunset Boulevard restaurant.

Immediately, Cliff Branson was signed to develop a screenplay based on Mineo's life and tragic death—stabbed to death as he parked his car behind his West Hollywood apartment in 1976—in which Tony would star. But after Tony's screen test proved that the only resemblance between Tony and Sal was physical, Natalie had been persuaded to shelve the project.

After that, no amount of pleading by Tony, backed by Rich Edwards—whom everyone but Natalie, apparently, knew had developed more than a professional interest in Tony—that Tony could be taught how to act dissuaded Natalie from plunging everyone at New Millennium Films into obtaining rights to *Smoking Out a Killer* and developing Roger Woolley's novel into a vehicle for Harry Hardin.

This switch in projects had been greeted by Nigel's enthusiastic approval on grounds of his conviction that no one would care to see a movie about a washed-up, admitted faggot—no matter how good-looking he was or how senseless his death.

The star dying in the last scene was box office poison! But how could anyone lose with a Harry Hardin film? Assuming, of course, Nigel thought, as he put on a fresh shirt, that Natalie came to her senses about firing Sheila Stevens, assuming that Harry would not carry out his threat to walk off the picture.

He looked at himself in a mirror. The shirt was fine. Should he put on a tie?

Looking at his wrist watch, he saw that it was nearly six. Tony had said dinner would be at seven. Lunch on the yacht had been hours ago.

Deciding against a tie, he left the room, hoping there'd be plenty of finger food with the drinks to carry him till eight.

Turning right, he came to Cliff Branson's door and knocked twice lightly.

Testifying to the nature of the owner of the house, three walls of Branson's south-facing room were adorned with posters of New Millennium Films productions: *A Grand Night for Murder, This One Will Slay You, A Killing on Wall Street,* and Natalie's latest film, and her only venture into a love story, last year's *Affair in Venice,* a financial bomb written by Sheila Stevens.

The main question now, thought Branson, as he opened the door to Nigel Wilson, was what were Natalie's intentions concerning Sheila's script for *Smoking Out a Killer*? There was no doubting that Natalie was not happy with the screenplay, but she'd made no mention of having decided to bring in another writer, namely, himself.

Grinning at Wilson, he blurted, "Nigel, I believe this is the first time I have ever seen you without a necktie. You look downright naked!"

As they passed the door to the room assigned to Richard Edwards and Parker Slade, they heard muted angry voices within.

"Not here an hour, and already they're having a lovers' spat," Branson said. "Shall we listen? I always enjoy a cat fight."

"Do what you wish," growled Nigel, striding ahead. "I need food and drink!"

Any chance of eavesdropping disappeared when a door opened farther down the corridor and Nick and Woolley emerged.

"Nigel, wait up," Branson said as the argument between Edward and Slade continued behind the door.

                              *   *   *

The row had started the moment Ivo Bogdanovich had left after escorting them to their room. Parker had slammed the door, turned round, and said in a demanding tone. "Admit it, you bastard, you've still got a hard-on for Tony Biciano."

"What are you talking about?"

"The minute you spied him on the dock in his tight white shirt and those cute shorts you couldn't keep your eyes off him. Did you think I wouldn't notice?"

What followed was ten minutes of silence and sulking.

Finally unable to stand it, Edwards said pleadingly, "Parker, you're imagining things. It was totally over between Tony and me months and months ago. Do you think I'd be carrying on with him after Natalie staked her claim? I've invested too much time and effort in New Millennium Films to jeopardize my career over a no-talent Sal Mineo wannabe. And you and I have come too far in this for you to put it all in jeopardy because you *think* I've still got the hots for Tony. Once this business with Natalie is settled, it's going to be clear sailing for me, and for your career. And then you will also see what Tony means to me when I hand Tony his head."

This had assuaged Parker until there was a knock on the door and Rich opened it to find Tony there. With a glance at Parker on the bed, he said, "Just checking to see if the arrangements are suitable."

"They're just fine, Tony," Rich replied nervously. "In fact, they're great."

"Good. See you for cocktails."

When he was gone, Parker was seething. "He was obviously hoping to find you alone."

The renewed argument continued as Nigel Edwards and Cliff Branson passed the door, followed by Nick and Woolley.

Hearing the angry voices and with a curious glance at the door, Woolley asked, "What do you make of that?"

"Professor, I long ago gave up speculating about what goes on in people's bedrooms."

"I don't trust those two."

"Is that because they're gay?"

"You've known me a long time, Nick. I am not homophobic."

"What don't you trust about them?"

"I don't like this business of a pornographic videotape."

"Have you seen it?"

"You know I haven't."

"How do you know it's pornographic?"

"Harry and Sheila said it is."

"You trust Harry and Sheila?"

"Yes, I do."

"Why?"

"Why not? They've been quite forthcoming and straightforward with us."

"Which is precisely why, my amiable and trusting friend, you should be cautious."

Twenty

THEY ENTERED A large parlor with comfortable-looking chairs and sofas. To the left of the doorway a line of bookcases was interrupted in the middle by a stone fireplace adorned by a slightly larger than life-size portrait of a younger Natalie Goodman. Wearing a floor-length red gown with a deeply scooped neckline enhanced by a diamond necklace, long white gloves, and a ruby bracelet on her left wrist, she had her eyes fixed on the opposite wall. Floor-to-ceiling glass, it afforded an ocean view and gave the room the effect of being suspended between sea and sky.

In front of the window stretched the bar. A long table converted for the occasion by Bill Restivo, it was covered with a red cloth and ranks of carefully arranged gleaming glassware of all sizes and shapes and what seemed to Nick to be a selection of kinds and brands of liquors that would have left Frankie-the-bartender at Farley's gaping with envy. Gathered before it were the guests who had preceded Woolley and Nick into the room.

"Shall we let the crowd thin out?" said Nick, moving to the picture. Looking up at it, he asked, "How old do you suppose she is in this painting?"

Woolley shrugged, "Thirty-something, probably."

"She'd certainly come a long way from sitting-in at the Copley Plaza."

"Times change and so do people."

Nick's eyes turned to the shelves of books. "She's evidently quite a reader. And catholic, small C, in her tastes. Histories, biographies, best-selling novels. And lots of mysteries. There you are, Professor! A complete collection of your Jake Elwell books. You're in very good company. Dashiell Hammett, Raymond Chandler, Arthur Conan Doyle, Mary Higgins Clark, and what appears to be the complete Nero Wolfe and all of Agatha Christie. I can see why the movies made by New Millennium Films are thrillers."

"You assume that all these books are hers," said Woolley. "They could have been collected by any one or all of her husbands."

"Of course. Why didn't I think of that?"

Woolley nodded toward the bar. "The crowd's thinned. Shall we?"

As they approached the bar, Harry Hardin turned from it, carrying two drinks. Flashing a smile at Nick, he held up both glasses. "Vodka martini, shaken, not stirred, for Sheila and Wild Turkey neat for yours truly. We're over there, as far from Natalie's picture and everyone else as possible, if you'd care to join us. But on second thought, Nick, you'll probably want to mix before Natalie makes a grand entrance. Isn't that what detectives are supposed to do? Mix in and eavesdrop on conversations?"

"Only in novels by Roger Woolley."

"Come and sit with Sheila and me," said Harry, walking away, "and we'll be happy to tell you all about everything. And everybody."

With Harry gone, Bill Restivo greeted Nick and Woolley with a bartender's smile. "Good evening, gentlemen. What may I serve you?"

Woolley surveyed the astonishing array of choices, then exclaimed, "I say! Do I really spy a bottle of Balluet cognac?"

"Mrs. Goodman says it's the prize of her wine cellar."

"I haven't seen Balluet cognac since I was last in France. Do you suppose she'd mind?"

"I'm sure she wouldn't."

Woolley pondered a moment. "No, I'd better ask her first. Let me have a scotch."

"Single malt or blended?"

"A Dewar's, I think."

"Straight? Water? Rocks?"

"A splash and one ice cube."

"I'll have a Jameson's," said Nick.

Restivo smiled knowingly. "Neat, of course."

Nick winked. "Is there any other way?"

With drink in hand, Nick surveyed the room. Harry and Sheila occupied a love seat that met the desired geographical criteria. Seated in two leather chairs in a corner on the far side of the room, Nigel Wilson and Simon Cane looked like a painting of members of an exclusive mens' club. Standing alone by a wall festooned with seascapes, Cliff Branson appeared to be studying an enormous picture of a storm-tossed clipper ship.

Nick whispered to Woolley, "I suggest you go one way and I go the other."

But before they could do so Edwards and Slade appeared in the doorway, hesitated for a moment, and strode hand in hand toward the bar.

"A truce seems to have been declared," Woolley observed.

"That's nice," said Nick, heading in Branson's direction. "I like happy endings." When he approached Branson, he said, "Natalie seems to be quite a collector of art."

"She collects, all right, but by the yard," Branson replied, still studying the picture. "I was here one day when she sent Tony Biciano and her decorator to scour the galleries in Portsmouth. The decorator had orders to buy sixteen paintings of his choice but of specified sizes. Tony had a briefcase full of cash. Naturally, when they returned to Pirate's Cove, all of the money was gone. But, I suspect, very little of it went for the paintings. Just look at this monstrosity."

"You think Tony and the decorator swindled her?"

"I never said so to Natalie, because she would not have believed it of Tony, even if I had been able to produce evidence. She was obsessed with him. She still is. That's Natalie's problem. She's blind to the possibility that someone she's placed her trust in could betray it. She is not the savvy businesswoman she would have you believe she is."

His eyes darted away from the painting toward Harry Hardin and Sheila Stevens.

Looking back to Nick, he continued in a whisper, "If Natalie were as sharp as she thinks she is, she wouldn't have bought into Rich Edwards's proposal that she sign fifteen-million-dollars-a-picture Harry Hardin."

"I thought Harry is a guarantee of a box office bonanza."

"He is, but only in a certain kind of film. People want Harry Hardin in action pictures, which *Smoking Out a Killer* certainly is not in the present script."

"It would have been different in the screenplay you wrote?"

"Definitely. No offense intended toward you and Mr. Woolley's book, but if the picture goes ahead with Sheila's adaptation, not even Harry Hardin will be able to pull in the grosses it will need to cover Harry's salary and points in order to make a respectable profit for New Millennium. A lot of people's careers depend on *Smoking Out a Killer* making up for the huge loss from *Affair in Venice* and putting the company back into the black. I wouldn't be surprised if that was why someone took a shot at Natalie a few nights ago."

"How would killing Natalie change anything?"

"Production has just begun. There's still time to avert a disaster."

"By going back to your original script?"

"That would certainly be a step in the right direction." He peered across the room and saw the maid enter, followed by Ivo Bogdanovich dressed as a waiter, each carrying a silver tray of appetizers. "Ah, here's food at last. I don't know about you, Nick, but I'm famished."

Ivo approached with a tray of water chestnuts wrapped

in bacon, dollops of diced crab on cracker wedges, creamed cheese on wafers, tiny quiche pies, caviar, and small, hot, Italian sausages the size of a man's little finger skewered with toothpicks.

Branson chose a quiche.

"Ivo, now you're a waiter," said Nick. "I'm beginning to think there is no limit to your range of talents. You are a veritable one-man show."

Ivo blushed a little. "I'm just lending a hand to Felicity."

"What man could fault you?" Nick said, going for the diced crab. "But I should warn you that Professor Woolley may be trying to beat your time."

Ivo laughed. "You're kidding me."

"Have you never heard the saying, 'Snow on the roof doesn't necessarily mean there's not a fire in the stove?' "

Still blushing, Ivo thrust the tray at Nick. "Try the sausage."

As Nick lifted one from the plate, there was a stir in the room.

Branson said, "Ah, the grand entrance."

Looking past Ivo, Nick watched Natalie sweep into the room. Her dress was royal blue. From a slender gold chain dangled a diamond and ruby seahorse.

"How wonderful," she said with a queenly wave of hand, "you're all here."

Like the heir-apparent prince, Tony Biciano, deeply suntanned and wearing a white polo shirt and gray slacks, entered two paces behind her.

Except for Harry Hardin and Sheila Stevens, Nick observed, the guests Natalie's memo had commanded to come to her island quickly formed a kind of reception line. First was Nigel Wilson, followed by Simon Cane. Then came Cliff Branson, bowing slightly. Richard Edwards and Parker Slade were next. Only then did Harry and Sheila leave their love seat and go to her. While Natalie greeted each guest with a handshake or an air kiss, Nick admired the poise of a woman who believed one or more of them had tried to kill her.

When all had demonstrated their obeisance, he watched

with amusement while Woolley rendered a courtly bow, raised her right hand, and kissed it. She responded with a laugh and a love tap to his cheek. "Professor, whatever would our former comrades in the revolution think?"

As Nick stood before her, she pretended their earlier meeting had not occurred. "It's good to see you, Nick. I trust you had a pleasant time on *Murder Two*?"

"I did."

"I'm looking forward to your talk on cigars after dinner tomorrow."

"I hope you won't be disappointed."

At seven o'clock Nick stood at the window watching *Murder Two* slip away from the dock as Tony Biciano came into the parlor and announced that dinner was ready.

In a large dining room overlooking the broad terrace Nora had set up a Down East-Maine buffet of New England clam chowder, immense boiled lobsters, buckets of steamed crabs, heaps of corn on the cob, and an array of fresh vegetables, cooked and raw. In contrast to this informality, a long table in the center of the room had eleven settings with place cards that had Natalie at the head, flanked by Woolley to the left and Nick to her right. Four other places on Nick's side of the table were assigned to Harry Hardin, then Richard Edwards, Simon Cane, and Sheila Stevens. More widely spaced on Woolley's side were Cliff Branson, Parker Slade, and Nigel Wilson. At the end opposite Natalie was Tony Biciano.

"Don't read anything into the seating, Nick," Natalie whispered as he took his place. "I put the names in a bowl and let fate choose, except for you and Woolley. I trusted neither of you would try to slip a bit of poison into my chowder."

"I assume that's also why you chose to have a buffet meal."

"Exactly. Anyone who might hope to poison me would have to poison all the food and, therefore, poison everyone."

"He, or she, wouldn't have to poison all the food. As for

killing everyone else, history is full of instances of someone willing to commit mass murder in order to kill one. Most of them have involved blowing up airliners in order to collect on an insurance policy or to cash in on an inheritance."

Assuming his place at that moment, Harry Hardin said, "Please, Nick, if you are going to tell stories about your personal war on crime, we'd all like to hear them."

Nick looked across the room at Woolley loading a dinner plate. "If it's tales of crime that you want, I prefer to leave the storytelling to the author of *Smoking Out a Killer* and a host of other titles for which I'm sure film rights are available."

"But Woolley writes fiction. How can that compare to the real thing?"

"In my experience, the real thing can be pretty dull stuff. Mrs. Smith finally gets fed up with Mr. Smith and finds the way out by grabbing a paring knife. Or a dope dealer eliminates the competition with a bullet. The reality of murder is that there's hardly ever any mystery involved. And when there is a case of a carefully plotted homicide, it's not solved by private sleuths like those we've all come to know and love that spring from the minds of an Arthur Conan Doyle, an Agatha Christie, and a Roger Woolley."

He appeared at that instant. "What's that about me?"

"I was telling Harry and Natalie that if they're interested in hearing true tales of murder and mayhem, there's no better authority than yourself. I cite, for instance, your encyclopedic knowledge of the murders on nearby Smutty Nose Island."

Seated, Woolley ignored his dinner. "What a ghastly event it was. Two helpless women hacked to death with an axe, and a third savagely wounded. But it's hardly the stuff for table talk!"

"On the contrary," said Natalie. "What could be better at a New England dinner than a story about a famous New England murder not three of four miles from where we sit?"

Woolley laid down the claw. "You're familiar with the case, Natalie?"

"One can't spend a minute in the Isles of Shoals," she

said, "and not be told about Louis Wagner's murderous rampage on Smutty Nose."

"It is, perhaps, because the murders occurred on a lonely island that the event is so long remembered," Woolley mused. "I vaguely recall someone who wrote about the Smutty Nose murders speculating on the incongruity of a place. An island at sea has always fascinated authors, from Homer to Defoe to Stevenson and the Benchley brothers, Nathaniel and Peter, sons of the Algonquin Round Table wit Robert Benchley. And of course, Agatha Christie, who put ten strangers on Indian Island and proceeded to have someone kill them according to a nursery rhyme."

Natalie interjected:

"Ten little Indian boys went out to dine;
One choked his little self and then there were nine.
Nine little Indian boys sat up very late;
One overslept himself and then there were eight."

Parker Slade blurted, "Didn't they make a movie of that?"

Nick replied, "*And Then There Were None*, with Barry Fitzgerald, Louis Hayward, Walter Huston, and Roland Young."

"No, no," Parker said, shaking his head. "*Ten Little Indians* had Hugh O'Brian and that old rock and roll guy, Fabian. I saw it once on the late show on TV. But it wasn't on an island. It was a snowed-in village somewhere in Europe."

"That was a remake," said Richard Edwards sharply. "And a not very good one."

"Remakes never are," said Nick.

"As a Christie fan," said Natalie, "I toyed with changing the name Pirate's Cove to Indian Island, but the local authorities wouldn't stand for it."

Harry asked, "Is it true that Blackbeard buried treasure around here?"

"I wish he had," Natalie replied. "I could have used it to finance building this house. But we're way off track. We're supposed to be hearing Professor Woolley's account of the murders on Smutty Nose." She placed a hand on Woolley's shoulder. "Please tell us the story."

Woolley abandoned his meal. "In March of 1873, two Norwegian immigrants, fishermen named John and Matthew Hontvet, their brother-in-law, Ivan Christensen, their wives, and a sister-in-law of the Hontvets, lived on Smutty Nose. . . ."

While the narrative continued, Nick's eyes wandered round the table as the guests recommended to him as suspects in a plot to kill Natalie Goodman both ate and listened.

Woolley described how a financially desperate German immigrant who had failed as a fisherman, Louis Wagner, with only the light from a sliver of moon to guide him as he rowed a small stolen boat across some twelve miles of ocean from Portsmouth to Smutty Nose, hoped to steal some money. Instead, he found himself murdering two women with an axe.

"Quickly caught and nearly lynched, convicted, condemned to hang, and after a daring but short-lived escape, Wagner appealed to the governor of Maine for mercy and clemency. 'Do I look like a murderer?' he asked the governor."

Nick's eyes surveyed the silent, rapt faces around the table and thought, "Who looks like a murderer?"

Woolley continued, "The governor looked Wagner up and down and replied, 'Louis, you look to me like a man that got himself in a corner and murdered his way out.' "

Nick thought, "Always the wrong thing to do."

"Louis Wagner was hanged for his crimes," Woolley continued. "The axe he is said to have used is on exhibit in a museum in Portsmouth."

Nick thought, "Proving again that crime doesn't pay."

A burst of applause from the suspects shook him out of his thoughts.

When quiet settled in the room, Natalie looked at the guests and said, "Since my dear old friend Professor Woolley has set a macabre tone, let's play a game. We'll call it

How I'd Kill Natalie This Weekend. You all take turns telling how, if you wanted to murder me, you would go about it. Nick will be the judge of who comes up with the cleverest method. But there is one exception. You may not choose shooting at me. That has been tried and, as you can all see, it failed. Who wants to go first?"

With stunned expressions, the guests looked at one another.

"No volunteers, I see," said Natalie. "Then I pick Professor Woolley to start."

"Natalie, darling," he said with a chuckle, "why would I want to kill you?"

"Don't spoil the game by being logical. How would you murder me?"

Woolley pondered a moment. "I would cut you down with my slashing wit!"

Everyone laughed nervously.

"One can always count on you to wiggle out of a tight spot with a clever retort," she said as she looked right and down the table at her attorney. "Simon, what about you?"

"Natalie, this is not amusing."

"I think it is. Permit me to answer for you. A lawyer's method would be to tie me up with legalisms and ironclad clauses until I'm unable to breathe. Is that about right?"

Cane smiled tightly. "If you say so."

"Yes, the client is always right. Sheila? Care to weigh in?"

"I think I'd collect every memo you've sent me, put them in a blender, add a dash of seasoning to mask the bad taste, stir it into a glass of your precious cognac, and watch you choke to death on your own venom."

Natalie's eyes shifted left. "The chair recognizes Nigel Wilson."

He squirmed a little. "I'd never wish you ill, Natalie."

"I expect your method would be death by a thousand paper cuts." As her gaze turned to Parker Slade, the handsome actor fidgeted and looked across the table at Rich Edwards. "And you, young man with stars in your eyes," she said, "would you act on your own, or would you prefer to share the credit?"

Edwards slapped a hand on the table, rattling the silver. "Damn it, Natalie, cut out all the teasing. If you believe one of us took a shot at you, say so. And while you're at it, explain to us why we've all been dragged up here."

Natalie's eyes went wide. "I wouldn't describe a voyage on my yacht as being dragged."

"You said in your memo there was business to be discussed. Well, let's get to it."

"But, dear, you've all just arrived. There's plenty of time remaining for business. Now, are you playing the game, Rich, or not?"

Edwards shot to his feet. "Not."

Natalie's eyes narrowed to slits. "Sit down and behave yourself."

Edwards resumed his seat.

"What is your answer? How would you choose to kill me?"

Edwards thrust out his hands. "With these. Slowly."

"Effective, but not very original."

Harry Hardin asked, "Is it my turn now, Natalie?"

"If you wish."

"Because I'm an actor and you are a producer, I think I would want you to suffer the way you've made Al Leibholz, Felix Marlowe, and so many others suffer. By that I mean publicly. So I think that I'd kill someone close to you—say, Tony."

Biciano rose halfway out of his chair. "You'd die trying."

"And then," Harry continued calmly, "I would find some means of framing you for it."

Natalie smiled. "Do you believe you're smart enough?"

"In my scenario you'd have the humiliation of an arrest and trial, and then you'd go to your death screaming your innocence. Of course, no one would hear, because of the applause. But I'd wait till after this picture was completed. I wouldn't want everyone's hard work wasted."

"The *noblesse oblige* of the superstar. How touching, Harry."

With a grin, Cliff Branson said, "I take it the limelight is now on me?"

"You always have been eager to get in the last word, Cliffie."

"I'd find a way," he said coolly, "so that you'd die at the box office."

"I'm afraid Sheila tried that method with *Affair in Venice*, but I'm still here." Turning to Nick, she said, "I won't ask you to render a judgment. But you do see, now, I hope, the difficulty in being a motion picture producer." She smiled benignly. "Now, shall we finish our dinner?"

PART VI

Roving Camera

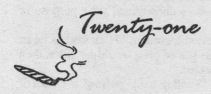

Twenty-one

DINNER OVER, NATALIE and Tony abruptly left the dining room without a word to anyone. Befuddled, bemused, shocked, and sullen guests quickly dispersed to their bedrooms. Felicity, Ivo, and Bill Restivo cleaned up.

Nick and Woolley went into the parlor to smoke.

"I have attended funerals that were more cheerful than that dinner," said Woolley as they sat in green leather armchairs. "Why do you suppose Natalie put on that appalling charade? She practically told them she thinks one of them is trying to kill her."

Nick took out a silver cigar clipper, a box of matches, and a leather pocket case containing four Dunhills. "As you've said to me several times," he said, offering Woolley one of the short, thick Coronas, "she's a remarkable woman."

Woolley declined the cigar, preferring a bent black briar pipe. Packing it, he said, "No one in his right mind would be so foolish as to try anything now."

"Taking a shot at Natalie last Sunday night was pretty foolish. But the purpose of this weekend in Natalie's mind is, to paraphrase the title of your book and Natalie's film, to smoke out a killer. She evidently hoped her game would catch someone off guard or that I might pick up a clue."

"Did you?"

Nick held the cigar above an ashtray and trimmed the end. "Let's just say that the exercise was not, as Sherlock Holmes would put it, without points of interest."

"It seems to me that she's undermined your purpose in being here."

"My purpose is to prevent a murder," Nick said as he lit up. "If Natalie's game has scared off a would-be killer, then a murder has been prevented."

"For now, perhaps," Woolley said, puffing a cloud of smoke. "But what about later?"

Nick got out of his chair and ambled over to the bookcases. "There's an increased urgency in this business, my friend," he said as he scanned the rows of books. "The California incidents were separated in time. The last two occurred a few hours apart. Natalie's game notwithstanding, I'm certain there will be another attempt this weekend. But it won't be tonight, I think."

"Is that so?"

"Obviously, Natalie will be spending the night in Tony Biciano's strong embrace. To kill her, you'd have to get him out of the way."

"That's what Harry Hardin said at dinner. In his scenario in Natalie's game he wouldn't kill Natalie. He'd kill Tony and frame Natalie for it."

"An interesting idea, but difficult to execute. If there is to be another try at murdering Natalie, it's not likely to happen when Tony's around. Besides, Natalie's game has put everyone on edge tonight. What do you recommend for a little bedtime reading?"

Woolley lit the pipe. "You can never go wrong with a mystery."

"The lady seems to own every one ever published."

"The Mystery Writers of America, of which I am proud to be a member, have a slogan," Woolley said, leaving his chair and going to the bookcases. " 'Any book worth reading is worth buying.' "

"I've read all of yours," Nick said, running a finger along the titles on the spines, "and the complete Holmes. What about a dash of Hammett?"

"This may be heresy, but I've always thought Hammett was better on the screen than on the page. The same for Raymond Chandler. And I've found that dear Dame Agatha's nosy old spinster from St. Mary Mead and the Belgian sleuth with the egg-shaped head have always been easier to take on film."

"Which actor do you think made the better Hercule Poirot? Peter Ustinov in *Death on the Nile* or Albert Finney in *Murder on the Orient Express?*"

"Finney," said Woolley, taking down a copy of the novel, "but no one could ever surpass David Suchet in the Poirot television series."

"In the Orient Express murder they all did it. Twelve people conspired to carry out an execution. Do you think it's possible that we're confronted with a conspiracy?"

Woolley returned *Murder on the Orient Express* to the shelf. "That would be much too complicated a trick to pull off."

"I've been told that the making of a movie is a collaboration."

"There would have to be a benefit for everyone in Natalie's death. In what manner would Harry Hardin benefit?"

"I gather he would get paid whether the film is completed or not, as long as he was not the reason the production ceased. If Natalie were killed and the project were scrapped, he would collect his salary and be free to move on to his next film. And he has an interest in what happens to Sheila Stevens."

"I grant you, Sheila has a plausible motive—to keep from being fired."

"An event that Natalie is taking her time about, if, indeed, that's what she intends."

"Assuming that is her aim, why would the man who is likely to take over for Sheila—"

"Cliff Branson."

Woolley fished a pipe tool from a pocket and proceeded to unclog the pipe's stem. "Why would Branson conspire to murder Natalie?"

"Revenge for having been humiliated?"

"What of Rich Edwards?"

"He's the heir apparent in the producing department, and he's obviously a good organizer of people. His lover would go along with the plan without question."

"Ambition, thy name is Parker Slade," said Woolley disgustedly. "The lawyer?"

"If you're going to conspire at anything, it's probably a good idea to have an in-house counsel. And Simon Cane is executor of Natalie's estate. He'd certainly know how to divide a financial pie seven ways."

With the pipe stem cleared, Woolley puffed a cloud of smoke. "Nigel Wilson?"

"Nigel appears to embrace all the classic motives for murder: love turned to hate, a need for revenge, greed, a hunger for status."

Nick took down Christie's *Witness for the Prosecution.*

"A prime example of a better movie than a book," said Woolley. "Charles Laughton as the barrister, Sir Wilfrid Robarts, was magnificent."

Nick replaced the book.

Woolley jerked the pipe from his mouth. "Tomorrow morning!"

Intent on his task, Nick removed the British edition of Christie's *The Mirror Crack'd from Side to Side.* "Wasn't this made into a movie?"

"Yes, starring Elizabeth Taylor and Rock Hudson. Jane Marple was played by Angela Lansbury."

"What about tomorrow morning?"

"Tony Biciano won't be around. He's going fishing."

"Yes, he is," Nick said, keeping the book.

"Natalie will be on her own."

"Which is why you will be getting up before six and going fishing, and I will not."

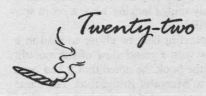

Twenty-two

"HAVE YOU ANY instructions for me for tomorrow?" Woolley asked as he opened the door to his room.

"Observe and listen," Nick replied. "And try not to fall overboard."

"Very funny, very funny indeed," Woolley huffed as he went in. "Enjoy your read. And if you intend to smoke a cigar, try not to set the bed on fire."

Closing his own door, Nick found the lights on. Looking around the bedroom, he listened to the house. Like Woolley, he had expected quite a different place. From the moment Natalie "blackmailed" him into spending a weekend on an island named Pirate's Cove, he'd envisioned something rustic, perhaps primitive—a kind of New England shore Baskerville Hall, dark and brooding and imbued with mystery, the roof, walls, and floorboards creaking in a nor'easterly wind. He had half hoped the island would be haunted not by a murderous hound, but by a pirate in search of his buried loot. Instead, he'd been conveyed in a luxury yacht to as modern and comfortable a house as he could imagine.

As if he were in a five-star hotel, the covers of the double bed had been turned down, presumably by Felicity Dane. The bag with his clothes and personal items and the paper sack containing cigars and cigar paraphernalia for his after-dinner talk, which had been delivered to the room by Ivo, had been placed on a window seat. When he looked in the drawer of a bureau, he found a pad of Pirate's Cove notepaper and a pen. The only things lacking were a room service menu and Gideon Bible.

Because he never smoked in bed, he chose to read in a chair by an open window with a grand view of the moonlit ocean. When he opened the book, he noted that it had been dedicated by the author to Margaret Rutherford. The name yanked him back in time to the 1960s and his wife. He'd taken Maggie and the two kids to all four of the movies that starred Rutherford as Miss Jane Marple. But only after Woolley had introduced him to Agatha Christie's amateur lady detective outsmarting the police in the pages of novels did he realize how Rutherford was physically miscast. Miss Marple in print was tall, thin, acidulated, and eventually restrained in movements by age. Margaret Rutherford was fat and jowly and always seemed to be on the run as she cracked the cases of *Murder She Said, Murder at the Gallop* (with roly-poly Robert Morley making a romantic pitch for her), *Murder Most Foul*, and his favorite of the four, *Murder Ahoy*, with Rutherford decked out in naval togs.

Reading, he soon found Miss Marple in her beloved garden, but too elderly now to do anything more than a little pruning. Deciding to go for a walk, she stumbled, literally, into an offer of tea from Heather Badcock and a gossipy hour about the new owners of Gossington Hall, a former movie queen named Marina Gregg and her husband, a film director. By coincidence, as seemed to be the norm in Agatha Christie stories, Jane later found herself investigating the mysterious death of Heather after she was taken ill while attending a benefit on behalf of a local hospital, held at Gossington Hall.

As much as he wanted to finish the novel, he eventually found the long day catching up with him. He felt very tired and sleepy. Since *Murder Two* had glided out of Boston Harbor, more than fourteen hours had passed and no attempt had been made to murder Natalie Goodman.

He yawned, stretched, and tossed the book onto the window seat. Undressing, he again listened to the house, but heard only the distant, gentle surging of the sea. Lying in bed, he welcomed sleep but found himself wondering what was happening in the other rooms, what was being said, and what were the thoughts of the people whose names he had first come to know by way of the list Natalie had given him at Farley's. Closing his eyes, he smiled and thought that if he were a movie detective, this scene of him lying in bed would slowly dissolve to another room, so that members of the audience could know more than the detective or be cinematically tricked into thinking they did.

Had such a device been available to Nick, the godlike omniscience of the camera would have revealed Rich Edwards and Parker Slade forgetting their earlier argument in a manner not likely to be approved by guardians of the motion picture code for a general audience. If such an explicit scene of intimacies between males were to make it onto the screen, the film would bear the dreaded X rating.

When Rich finished, Parker looked down at him and said, "You were supposed to settle our problem with Natalie tonight."

Rich raised his head. "How could I? With Tony glued to her, I couldn't get near Natalie. But remember what Scarlett O'Hara said in *Gone with the Wind*. Tomorrow is another day."

Parker lit a cigarette. "He'll be glued to her then, too."

"No, no, my boy. Tomorrow is Tony's big fishing excursion."

If a camera had been rolling at that moment in Harry Hardin's bedroom, it would have found him and Sheila Stevens recovering from the same activity that had engaged Edwards and Slade, but with Harry smoking the cigarette.

"I really expected Natalie to announce at dinner that she's firing you," he said. "I wonder what she's waiting for? Maybe she's changed her mind."

"As long as I've known her," Sheila said, sitting up, "she's played her little games."

"The one she pulled from her hat at dinner was really bizarre. I thought your answer about giving her a poisonous potion made from her memos was brilliant."

Sheila left the bed for the bathroom. "Yours about killing Tony and framing Natalie for it was good, too."

Elsewhere in the house, a camera would have found Simon Cane, briefcase opened on the bed, speaking on the phone to the man he had barely missed in his earlier call to his offices.

If Leiberman resented having been awakened in the wee hours of a Saturday morning, he did not say so to Cane as he related the details of the pretrial conference that Cane had been forced to forgo by Natalie Goodman's outrageous edict.

"I was hoping to be able to get off this damned island and back to New York tomorrow," Cane said, "but until this business is cleared up, I have to stick around."

In the room next to Cane's, Nigel Wilson was seated at a dressing table.

Spread before him were papers and reports containing details of the costs so far accrued in making *Smoking Out a Killer*.

He had hoped by now to have found a moment to go over the alarming numbers with Natalie. But an attempt to do so immediately after the yacht had arrived had been rebuffed by Tony Biciano.

In his snottiest tone, Tony had said, "When Natalie is ready to talk business with you, Nigel, I'll be the one to let you know."

Two doors down and across the long corridor from Wilson's room, Clifford Branson was reading a revised screenplay. If all went as planned, it would soon go from paper to film.

*   *   *

Close to the kitchen in a small, spartan room with twin beds that Ivo Bogdanovich was sharing with Bill Restivo, the talk was of Tony Biciano's promise that if Bill's service as the bartender for this weekend proved satisfactory, Bill would be given a part in the movie. Bill had asked Ivo if Tony could be taken at his word.

Ivo had replied, "He's always kept his word to me."

"But does he have that much influence with Natalie?"

"Let me put it this way," Ivo said. "If Tony tells Natalie to give you a part in the picture, you're in the movie."

Bill's eyebrows knitted into a frown. "She puts that much faith in his judgment?"

Ivo's brows went up devilishly. "It's not what Natalie puts into Tony," he said through a cackling laugh, "it's what Tony puts in her."

Bill flashed a lewd grin. "So have you put the moves on the maid yet?"

"Hey! I just got here a couple of hours ago! With a girl like that you gotta go slow."

"A word of advice, Ivo. Felicity is not the sweet and innocent thing you think she is."

"How do you know? You only just met her yourself."

"Yeah, but I've seen plenty of that type. Of both genders. I can always spot somebody who's on the make. That girl definitely is."

"Everybody's on the make for something."

"My advice to you is to watch out you don't get run over in the process."

Ivo shrugged. "Don't worry about me. I know how to handle women."

"If the time comes that you want this room for an hour, you just let me know and I'll make myself scarce."

"If I do want the room, it won't be for a measly hour."

"Maybe you should try scratching at Felicity's door right now."

"Unfortunately, she's sharing a room with Nora."

"That woman may look like a battleship, but she is a *great* cook."

*   *   *

In their shared quarters, Nora and Felicity were sound asleep with Nora's alarm clock set for a quarter after five so that she could prepare breakfast for those guests who had decided to go deep-sea fishing with Tony.

Twenty-three

As NORA ROSE and shook Felicity Dane awake, the trim fishing smack *Clara Bella* with Bob Gibson at the wheel was skirting the north side of Pirate's Cove. The last time he'd been called to the island, he recalled, was to pick up likable Stanley Goodman, a fisherman after his own heart. Then the house on the island was a ramshackle thing tucked between the remnants of the old missile base. But after he died, all that was soon gone, and in its place stood the virtual palace that had been built by his widow.

The one time Gibson had seen Natalie, she was pointed out to him by Nora Swanson in Portsmouth. He had found her a strikingly handsome woman. A strong-willed and a demanding employer, according to Nora, who did the cooking when Mrs. Goodman was in residence, which was not so often. But she was not interested in fishing, which was why he had been surprised when a young man who didn't look much like a fisherman showed up in Portsmouth looking to charter a boat and all the necessary equipment for a Saturday in August.

The sound of the boat's motor through an open window drew Nick out of bed. He had been awake for half an hour, thinking about the previous day and the remarkable dinner that had capped it. Standing at the window, he took in a view of a cloudless sky, a placid, sun-flaked sea, and the approach of the boat. Watching it ease to the dock, he heard voices in the hallway but could not identify them. A few moments later, there was a knock on the door.

Donning a blue robe that had been Maggie's last Christmas gift to him, he opened the door and found Woolley dressed for fishing in a denim shirt, blue jeans, thick-soled boots, and the same white cap. "Well, well," Nick said, "if it isn't Captain Ahab!"

"Marvelous day," Woolley exclaimed. "You slept well, I hope?"

"Like a top."

"Have you had your breakfast? I've had mine. Nora's laid out a marvelous spread in the dining room."

"I'll check it out later."

"Are you sure you won't join us today?"

"I've made no change in plan, Professor."

"At least you can come and see us off."

"I'll be down in a few minutes."

When he arrived, he found Woolley, Harry Hardin, Cliff Branson, Rich Edwards, Ivo Bogdanovich, Bill Restivo, and Tony Biciano observing the docking of the boat.

"Boys only, I see," he said to no one in particular.

Tony turned and asked, "Have you changed your mind, Nick? There's plenty of room."

"Thanks, but I'm strictly a landlubber. How's Natalie?"

"Never better."

"I thought she'd be down to see you all off."

Tony turned toward the house and pointed to Natalie at a window. "She told me that if I saw you, to tell you she hopes you'll join her for breakfast in her office at seven o'clock."

Nick waved at the figure in the window.

As he turned back, he saw Woolley talking to the boat's leathery-faced skipper.

"I see you've named her the *Clara Bella*," he said as Gibson looped a rope around a piling. "The name is somehow familiar to me."

"She's named after the schooner that belonged to a fisherman whose wife and another woman were butchered on Smutty Nose Island. I use her sometimes to take tourists there."

"This is splendid! I was hoping to find someone to take me over there."

"I'd be happy to, sir. When would you like to go?"

"I'm here only for the weekend, so it would have to be tomorrow."

"Very good, sir. We can make the arrangements while we're out today."

Woolley turned to Nick with an anxious look. "Will that be okay with you? My making a jaunt to Smutty Nose won't interfere with your plans?" When Nick glanced anxiously at the others, Woolley feared he'd said too much.

"As you said, Professor," Nick said with a patient smile, "you can't be close to Smutty Nose without visiting it."

Gibson declared, "Time to be gettin' on board, folks."

Back in his room, Nick passed the time before breakfasting with Natalie by reading a little more of the Christie novel. At five before seven he made his way toward her office, passing the dining room, where Felicity Dane was serving breakfast to Nigel Wilson and Simon Cane.

Pausing in the doorway, he said, "Good morning, gentlemen. I hope you both slept as well as I did. Nothing like sea air, right?"

Without looking up, Cane muttered something indistinguishable.

Wilson put down a fork, looked at Nick sternly, and demanded, "Just what, may I ask, is your business with Natalie?"

Nick smiled. "Let's just say that I'm a guy who never could turn down an invitation to spend a weekend on an island with a beautiful woman. Enjoy your breakfast, gentlemen."

When he knocked twice on Natalie's door, she said, "Come in, Nick."

He entered and found her behind her desk. Two breakfast

trays, a silver coffee service, cups, glasses and a pitcher of orange juice stood upon it.

"How'd you know it was me?"

"Only a man knocks like that."

"I'm not the only man in this house."

"You're the only one who knows I'm in the office. Pull up a chair. Nora has brought us a wonderful breakfast."

"That was quite a game you sprang on everyone last night."

"You disapproved?"

"I think it was a very foolish thing to do."

Natalie poured two cups of coffee. "No one has dared to call me foolish since my last husband. That's what I like about you, Nick. With you it's full speed ahead and damn the torpedoes. As to the game, everyone at that table knows someone is trying to kill me. I thought it would be fun to let them know that I also know it and am not frightened."

"You might well have ruined any chance I had of finding out if the person who's been making these attempts is one of them," said Nick, digging into the eggs. "You've probably also delayed any attempt that might have been made during this weekend."

"You are wrong there, Nick." She opened the center drawer of the desk and took out a sheet of paper. "Tony found this slipped under my bedroom door this morning."

In large black print made with a felt-tipped pen on Pirate's Cove notepaper it read:

THE TIME FOR FUN AND GAMES IS OVER

Nick folded the note and slipped it in a pocket. "This sort of thing is out of a bad movie."

"You're dealing with people who work in movies, Nick."

"You're taking this seriously?"

"Why shouldn't I?"

"Someone is turning the tables on you for your joke in asking each of them to say how he or she would kill you. This is tit for tat."

"If you say so. You are the detective. I hope you've

found the accommodations here on the island to your liking."

"One thing's for sure," he said, picking up a strip of crisp bacon, "you've got plenty of books to read. You're quite a collector of the mystery genre."

"That's primarily the work of my late husband. Stanley introduced me to the delights of the thriller. He adored Agatha Christie. There's one of her novels that I wanted to make into a film until I found out it had been done. What fascinated me was that Christie based the novel on an incident in the life of the actress Gene Tierney. It seems that while she was pregnant, Tierney was exposed to a woman who had German measles. The child was born deaf, nearly blind, and mentally retarded. Christie's book has a similarly unfortunate actress get even by murdering the person who had infected her, unwittingly, of course. Christie had a penchant for lifting plots from items in the news."

"Professor Woolley claims that Agatha Christie used up all the good plots. But as interesting as it is to talk about books and movies, I don't think that's why you wanted to see me."

"I wanted to show you the note. Although you think it's of no importance, I would like to know who left it. Is such a thing possible?"

"Probably, but not without the facilities of a police crime laboratory and a forensic graphologist and documents analyst."

"Couldn't you get everyone together, make them write out the words in that note, and then make a comparison?"

"I doubt that whoever wrote the words would be so stupid as to duplicate the original. And I assume that the notepaper can be found in every bedroom. It's a very nice amenity."

"Placing notepads in the rooms was Tony's idea. He thinks of things that would never occur to me. It was his idea to arrange for the fishing boat. He also suggested the yacht to bring all of you here. He thought it would provide you with an opportunity to observe the suspects."

"Has he expressed an opinion as to who's trying to kill you?"

"He believes it's Rich Edwards."

"Did he tell you why he thinks so?"

"Tony regards Rich as a ruthless person who will let nothing stand in the way of his ambition to take control of New Millennium Films."

"Do you look at Rich that way? Ruthless, I mean?"

"Ruthlessness is what New Millennium needs. As to Rich casting an eye on the company, I've stuck my thumb in that optic many times. Rich is too impatient."

"How does Rich feel about Tony Biciano? Does he see Tony as a competitor?"

"I assume so."

"Is there any basis for that?"

"I have a great deal of confidence in Tony, but my plans for him do not include turning over the company to him. As I told you, I hope to marry him. Should I do so, I have no intention of sharing him with the movie business. I expect to do a great deal of traveling. That's one reason why I bought the yacht."

"Tony understands this?"

"Perfectly. I'm a wealthy woman, Nick. I've taken steps that in time will make Tony a richer man than he could ever hope to become in the picture business, except by becoming a new Harry Hardin. Tony has the looks and the body to be an action-film star, but he doesn't have the requisite acting talent. Tony understands that. He's a very sweet boy and very protective of me, especially since this unpleasantness began."

"Yet he's left you alone today."

"He knew you'd be here."

"What if I'd gone out on that boat?"

"I knew you wouldn't, just as I knew when I invited you to dinner at Farley's that you would not decline to come up here for this weekend."

"You must think you understand me pretty well."

"How could I not know you? I read Woolley's book."

"I doubt that any of your guests is buying the story that

I'm here to entertain and educate them by talking about cigars."

"Perhaps I was a trifle naive on that score."

"Does that mean I can skip putting on a dog and pony show?"

"You may, if you wish, but I'll be very disappointed. I've been looking forward to it. I'm very fond of cigars."

"Most women say they stink."

"My three husbands were cigar smokers, so I suppose I've gotten used to the aroma. If that makes me a rarity among women, so be it. Now, suppose you and I concentrate on having our breakfast. If Felicity carries untouched trays back to the kitchen, Nora will be insulted."

"What are you plans for the day?"

"I've got a mountain of work to do. I promise you I shan't leave this room until cocktail time. By then Tony will be back to watch over me."

PART VII

Cigars after Dinner

Twenty-four

SATURDAY MORNING PASSED at a leisurely pace with Nick on the terrace. Ensconced in a big white wicker chair with navy-blue cushions, he entered into the company of Miss Jane Marple and Chief Inspector Dermot Eric Craddock as they investigated the mystifying death of Mrs. Badcock at Gossington Hall. Around ten o'clock, as he smoked an H. Upmann Corona, he discovered that the title of the novel was taken from a line in Alfred, Lord Tennyson's "The Lady of Shalott":

> Out flew the web and floated wide;
> The mirror crack'd from side to side;
> "The curse is come upon me!" cried
> The Lady of Shalott.

Like English gentlemen of Tennyson's time, Nick mused, as he set aside the book and gazed out at the water, the writer had been a pipe smoker, thanks to the introduction of Virginia tobacco to England by Sir Walter Raleigh. Because Spanish and Portuguese explorers of the New World had concentrated their efforts in Cuba and the West Indies, they had carried back to their homelands the way of smoking of the indigenous population of the islands—the cigar.

History and the fortunes of nations, someone had written, was geography.

Nick held out the cigar he was smoking and looked at it admiringly.

Author John Galsworthy said, "By the cigars they smoke, ye shall know the texture of men's souls."

And Rudyard Kipling wrote a poem in which a young man was given an edict by his betrothed, Maggie, that if he were to marry her, he would have to give up cigars.

In Kipling's classic the youth replied:

> *Open the old cigar-box,—let me consider anew,—*
> *Old friends, and who is Maggie that I should*
>   *abandon you?*

If Maggie would not take him and his cigars, there were other women who would:

> *A million surplus Maggies are willing to bear*
>   *the yoke;*
> *And a woman is only a woman, but a good cigar*
>   *is a Smoke.*

Thinking ahead to the evening, Nick wondered if he should quote Kipling. How much of the history of cigars and cigar smoking ought he to include in his after-dinner talk—if any. Natalie had not provided any guidance. Did she expect him to provide a comprehensive tutorial on the many kinds, shapes, sizes, and characteristics of cigars? Books had been written on such subjects. How much could he cram into a few minutes?

What about the man at the Dunhill store in London telephoning Winston Churchill after a German bombing raid and telling the Prime Minister not to worry, his stash of cigars had survived? Mark Twain vowing that if Heaven did not allow cigar-smoking he would prefer to go to Hell. The fat man, Guttman, offering Sam Spade a Corona Del Ritz in *The Maltese Falcon*. President John F. Kennedy ordering an embargo on importation of Cuban cigars only after he was assured by his press secretary, Pierre Salinger, that the White House had been stocked with a thousand of JFK's favorite H. Upmanns.

Picking up his book and placing the cigar in his mouth, Nick thought, "There is more to smoking a cigar than anyone who has never smoked one could ever appreciate."

Whatever he decided to say after dinner did not really matter. The truth of the situation confronting him was that his talk on cigars was irrelevant. The talk was a ruse.

He placed the Christie novel face down on a table and looked out to sea. Two of Natalie's suspects—Richard Edwards and Clifford Branson—were on board the *Clara Bella* with Woolley, Tony, Harry, Ivo, and Bill Restivo. For the moment they were in no position to murder anyone, except, perhaps, a few fish.

Simon Cane and Nigel Wilson were visible through opened French doors, seated apart in the parlor. Sheila Stevens was not far away on the terrace, wearing a colorful sleeveless dress and stretched out on her back on a chaise longue, sunning herself. In a deck chair a few feet away in a skimpy swimsuit handsome Parker Slade was working on his tan.

Natalie, if she remained true to her word, was in her office.

One of the two others on the island for the weekend, pretty Felicity Dane, appeared at Nick's side, carrying a tray of tall glasses and a large pitcher with ice cubes floating in something.

"Excuse me, sir," she said. "Nora said to tell you that lunch will be served in the dining room at noon. She also made lemonade. Would you like some?"

"I would indeed." As Felicity poured, he asked, "Is Mrs. Goodman still in her office?"

"I believe so, sir. Can I bring you anything else?"

Nick took the glass. "Thank you, no."

As Felicity moved away to serve Sheila Stevens and Parker Slade, Nigel Wilson came out of the parlor and strode purposefully in Nick's direction. Looming above Nick, he asked, "May I have a word with you, Mr. Chase?"

"Of course. Mind if I smoke?"

"Certainly not," Wilson said, drawing up an identical wicker chair. "I'm not a member of the smoke police."

"These days," Nick said, taking a puff, "you never know."

"Mr. Chase, I'm a direct man," Wilson said.

"Good. I like a man who's direct."

"I must demand that you explain why you are here."

Nick sipped lemonade. "I was invited."

"Yes, of course. But why?"

"You'll have to ask Natalie."

"Is she your client?"

"I don't have clients, Mr. Wilson. I have customers. I run a cigar store."

"You are also a detective."

"I used to be. But if I were still a detective, what reason could there be for Natalie to invite me to take part in what so far has been a delightful weekend?"

"You could have been invited in order to conduct an investigation."

"An investigation into what?"

Wilson looked round, pulled his chair closer, and whispered, "Into some irregularities of a financial nature. Very high-tech stuff."

"It's been years since I worked on the frauds and bunko squads. Back then it was mostly a paper chase. These days it's software. I wouldn't know one end of a computer from the other. But if you're aware of a fraud taking place in Natalie's affairs, you should go to the police."

"At first, all I had was a suspicion."

"Have you spoken to Natalie about it?"

"Several times. That's why I supposed she'd turned to you."

"Assume for moment that she did. What would you have to say that might interest me?"

"As I said, I had only a suspicion at first."

"You keep saying 'at first.' When was that?"

"A few months ago, shortly after Natalie acquired the

rights to Woolley's novel, I saw a preliminary budget that looked very irregular."

"I've heard that in Hollywood irregular-looking budgets are pretty regular."

"Indeed so, which is why I did nothing about my misgivings. However, last night, when I was reviewing the picture's current financial status, I found the situation even more troubling."

"In what way?"

"I've detected a pattern of manipulation by an individual to divert funds to himself. He's been very clever about it. But it's there."

"And the individual doing the manipulation is?"

Wilson leaned close and whispered directly into Nick's ear. "Richard Edwards."

"Have you informed Natalie?"

"I wasn't positive until last night. I planned to speak to her this morning, but she's locked herself in her office. I've knocked several times, but she refused to open the door. She told me in no uncertain terms to go away."

"I happen to know she has a lot on her mind this morning."

"I was hoping that if you spoke to her about what I've told you, she'd hear me out."

"Have you shared your suspicions with anyone else?"

"Certainly not."

"Good. Keep it that way."

Wilson leaned back and smiled. "I knew I was correct about you, Mr. Chase. You have been brought here as a detective."

"As you will find out after dinner this evening, Mr. Wilson," Nick said, rolling his cigar between thumb and forefinger, "I'm only here to talk about cigars."

Twenty-five

THIS CERTAINLY IS an odd lot, thought the skipper of *Clara Bella* as she rode at anchor about five miles due east of Pirate's Cove. Since they were guests of Mrs. Goodman, he'd expected an older group. But now that he'd met them, he supposed that they were friends of the young man who'd booked the charter.

He'd spent four hours observing them. Friendliest by far was Ivo. Short and stocky, he looked Russian, but at some point Ivo had told him that he was of Croatian extraction and some of his relatives in the old country were fishermen. Least likable was the one called Rich—a fairy if he'd ever seen one, although he tried to hide it. Arrogant, as well. The one who seemed most interested in learning how to fish was named Cliff. He remarked that he was some kind of writer and maybe he'd write a story about commercial fishing. This comment brought a crack from a ruggedly handsome, slightly older guest in a canary-yellow shirt that Cliff shouldn't waste his time because no one could possibly top Spencer Tracy in *Captains Courageous*.

The only natural fisherman in the bunch was the oldest—seventy, at the least—whom they addressed as Mr. Woolley. Although he was way overdressed, in the first two hours no one but him had hooked anything, a really fine flounder. The rest proved to be so squeamish about baiting hooks or so inept in handling the rods that he wondered why they had come along. Even the young man, Tony, who'd chartered the boat appeared ill at ease and kept looking at his watch, as if he had a schedule to keep.

At noon they all seemed relieved when the young man named Bill announced a break for a lunch that he'd brought on board in several wicker baskets and coolers.

When Woolley took a sandwich and a bottle of beer and went off by himself to the bow, Gibson grabbed a ham and cheese on a roll and followed him.

"I never take *Clara Bella* out," he said as he sat beside Woolley, "that I don't say the old salt's prayer, 'Oh, Lord, thy sea is so great and my boat is so small.' I'm told that President John F. Kennedy kept those words framed on a wall in the White House. JFK was a man who loved the sea. He was in the navy during the war. And quite a fisherman, too."

"Are you a student of presidents, Mr. Gibson, or just those who like the water?"

"I'd never vote for a man for president who wasn't a fisherman. That's why I could never go for Nixon. Maybe if Nixon had spent some time fishing and hanging around with fishermen, he wouldn't have had to resign in disgrace."

"Do you have a favorite fishing president?"

"I liked Harry Truman a lot, mostly because he went deep-sea fishing when he took his vacations down in Key West. Herbert Hoover said that for every hour a man spends fishing the Good Lord forgives one sin. When you've been taking folks fishing for as long as I have, you can spot right away the ones who have the right stuff. Take the late Mr. Goodman. You couldn't find a fella who lived up to President Cleveland's standard more than he did. He tried so hard to get his wife interested, but it wasn't her cup of tea. I was surprised as hell when that young man, Tony what's-his-name, came into Portsmouth and said she'd sent him to see if he could charter *Clara Bella* for today."

"I suppose she thought her guests would enjoy a fishing excursion."

"Maybe, but as far as I know, this is the first time she's done so since she built the big new house, and I know from Nora, her cook, that she's had lots of guests in that time. Is it true what I've heard from Nora that Mrs. Goodman is a movie producer?"

"She is indeed. The people on your boat are involved in her current production. In fact, one of them is the star of the picture."

"Really? Which one?"

"The young man wearing the yellow shirt."

"He's a movie star? He looks like an ordinary guy. I thought maybe it would be Tony, who chartered the boat. He's a lot better looking."

"Tony is Mrs. Goodman's . . . assistant."

Gibson thought a moment about Woolley's slight pause before the word "assistant." With a sly smile, he said, "Okay, I think I get your meaning. What about you?"

"What about me?"

"Are you in the show business?"

"I'm a retired professor of history and literature."

"Where'd you learn to be such a good fisherman?"

"I wouldn't say that I am. But I used to do a lot of fishing when I visited a friend, now deceased, who had a cottage on Cape Cod."

"Plenty of good fishing in those parts. What kind of movies does Mrs. Goodman make?"

"I believe the term is 'action pictures.' That's why Harry Hardin is starring. He's tops in action films these days."

"Do you think he'd mind if I asked for his autograph?"

"I'm sure he'd be happy to give you one."

"What's the name of the movie you're making?"

"*Smoking Out a Killer.* It's based on a book of that name."

"I'll try to see it when it comes out. When will that be?"

Woolley pondered the reason Nick had come to Pirate's Cove. If whoever was trying to kill Natalie Goodman were to succeed, would the picture ever be completed?

"I don't know when it will be released," he replied. "Filming has only just started."

*   *   *

In midafternoon a shelf of dark-gray clouds slid over the boat from the northwest, and the wind picked up. With the water turning choppy and the *Clara Bella* pitching and rolling, Gibson declared, "We'd best be gettin' back in, folks."

The catch for the day was four, Woolley's being the largest.

Gazing at them in a basket, Harry Hardin chuckled and said to him, "I hope Nora isn't planning on them for our dinner. I'm sorry Nick didn't come along. He might have done better."

"I seriously doubt that. Nick is not an outdoors guy."

"The cerebral type? Like Sherlock Holmes? Catching criminals using pure brain power?"

"I'm sure he did a good deal of that when he was with the New York City police. Nick's not one to sit around and tell war stories."

Harry gave a pat to Woolley's back. "He leaves that to his version of Dr. Watson."

Woolley peered up at the darkening sky. "We seem to be in for a blow."

Harry also studied the ominous-looking clouds. "The scene: Night time. Exterior. Establishing shot of Drearcliff Manor. A storm is raging. Slow dissolve to the interior of the house. The camera roams the shadowy great hall. As it comes in for a closeup of a door, a shot rings out. A woman screams. A body falls to the floor. Cut to the interior of a warm and cozy tobacco shop where the proprietor, a retired detective, is lighting a cigar." He looked sidelong at Woolley. "Or should it be a pipe? No, it is definitely a cigar. Ever since Basil Rathbone in all those Sherlock Holmes films, the pipe-smoking detective is a cliché."

"What about a cigarette?"

"Bogart took out the patent in *The Maltese Falcon.*"

"In addition to being a movie star, you are quite a writer, Harry. But why must it be the scream of a woman?"

"In movies like this, Professor, a man never screams. For terror you want a high-pitched voice. In the famous shower scene in *Psycho*, Janet Leigh screamed her head off, aided by sound effects and music. But when Martin Balsam was attacked with a knife at the top of the stairs, he uttered not a sound. You have got to hand it to Alfred Hitchcock. He knew a thing or two about how to scare the wits out of people."

"What a fascinating business you're in."

Harry looked skyward again as a light rain began. "I wouldn't be surprised if Natalie ordered up these really terrific special effects."

Woolley turned up the collar of his coat and pulled down the brim of his cap. "Do movie producers have the power to give orders to Mother Nature?"

"Most of them want to you to believe they do."

Thunder rolled dully in the distance.

Harry draped an arm across Woolley's shoulder. "Just between you, me, and the special effects, my friend, who does Nick suspect is trying to kill Natalie? And don't try to hand me that story about Nick being here to give us all a lecture on cigars. Nobody believes it."

"Believe what you will," said Woolley, turning to seek shelter in the boat's cabin, "but it's the truth."

Harry followed Woolley inside. "You should be an actor, Professor. You learn your lines and stick to them." He looked at the others and asked, "How many of you guys believe that Nick Chase has been invited among us just to teach us about cigars? Excluding Professor Woolley and Bill Restivo, who I'm sure has no idea what I'm talking about, a show of hands, please."

Ivo and Tony raised theirs.

Harry looked at Branson. "Cliff, what do you say Nick's real purpose is?"

"Natalie thinks one of us is trying to kill her. Nick's job is to find out which one."

"Of course," said Rich Edwards with an emphatic nod.

"There you are, Professor," said Harry. *"Vox populi."*

"As is so often the case in history," Woolley said, sitting on a bench, "the voice of the people is wrong."

"Do you deny," said Edwards, "that Natalie asked Nick

to come along on this weekend outing after someone shot at her in Boston?"

"I know for a fact that Nick was invited earlier."

"That's true," said Tony Biciano. "Nick didn't know about Natalie being shot at until she spoke to him right after it happened."

"And why," said Edwards excitedly, "did Natalie feel the need to tell him?"

"She knew he'd hear about it. The police were called. Reporters came. It was going to be on the news and in the papers. She wanted to inform him about the incident herself and to tell him that her plan for the weekend was unchanged."

"It was a plan, all right," Edwards said. "It was a plan in which Nick was expected to find out who is behind these attempts on her life."

"Attempts?" Woolley asked. "I'm only aware of the shot fired outside her hotel, if, in fact, it was aimed at her."

"Of course it was," Edwards answered. "Just as the light that fell over was aimed at her."

Woolley grunted. "Speculation."

"Somebody's trying to kill Natalie and she knows it."

Edwards nodded agreement. "That's why she pulled that stunt at dinner last night."

"She staged that game," Branson asserted, "because Nick was there to observe us, to see how we reacted."

Harry blurted a laugh. "It was a device straight out of a Nick and Nora Charles movie."

"It was a game, a silly one, I grant you," Woolley replied, "but why would Natalie suspect one of you or any of the others at dinner last night of wanting to kill her? And if she did suspect one of you, why wouldn't she report her suspicion to the police? Why would she ask for the help of a man who's been retired from detective work for more than fifteen years?"

"You know the answer to that question better than any of us, Professor," said Edwards. "She read a certain bestselling book about just such a person."

Woolley forced a laugh. "I can hardly wait to tell Nick

of this conversation. I assure you, he'll be most amused. And I expect so will Natalie. Now may we talk about something else?"

"You're not getting off that easily," said Branson. "Forget about whether Nick is or isn't playing detective for Natalie. I'm interested in knowing from a professional mystery writer which of us would be the most likely suspect if, Heaven forbid, Natalie is murdered."

"Now who's playing a macabre game?"

"That's a dodge, Professor."

"Very well, if you insist," Woolley said, looking from one to another. "If I created such a situation as this in one of my Jake Elwell novels, he would follow the well-trodden path of the detective genre and go after the least likely character. Namely Ivo Bogdanovich."

Ivo gasped. "Me?"

Everyone else laughed.

"I'm sorry, Ivo," Woolley said, "but I couldn't resist."

"All right, Professor," said Edwards. "Since you're unwilling to give away the plot, we'll just have to let the drama play out."

With everyone falling silent, Bob Gibson thought they were the queerest bunch of people he'd ever seen.

By the time he docked *Clara Bella* at Pirate's Cove, the storm was in full roar.

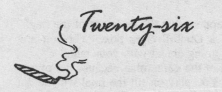

Twenty-six

THREE HOURS AFTER returning from the fishing expedition, Woolley had taken a refreshing nap and was now in dry clothing, smoking a pipe, and gazing through the window of Nick's room at a tempest showing no sign of subsiding.

"What a storm! It's amazing how fast it came up. One minute the sun was shining, the sea calm, and in the next—" He turned and looked at Nick removing cigar boxes from a paper bag. "I'm worried about Mr. Gibson. I pleaded with him not to attempt sailing back to Portsmouth. He laughed and told me not to worry."

"I'm pretty sure he's dealt with worse storms than this one."

Woolley again looked at the dark and churning sea. "I understand now how in the old days ships would find themselves suddenly caught in such weather and driven onto rocky shores and breaking up." He puffed a cloud of smoke. "What bravery!"

"You haven't told me how it went today."

Woolley removed the pipe from his lips and beamed. "I caught a huge flounder."

"I wasn't referring to fishing. What was the atmosphere, the attitude, among the men?"

Woolley left the window and sat at the foot of Nick's bed.

"They are convinced you are here because Natalie engaged you to find out who's trying to kill her. They do not buy into the story that Natalie invited you to educate them about cigars."

"Yes, well, it does appear that the cat's out of the bag."

Woolley picked up a Dunhill cigar box. "Yet you are obviously intent upon going ahead with your talk."

"One doesn't abandon the game plan because the opponent has found it out. You play on till the final whistle."

"Surely you don't expect anything to happen now?"

"I'd be a damned fool not to."

From the bottom of the bag he drew a handful of plastic cigar clippers for use in his demonstration of the proper techniques of cigar smoking.

"Now, what do you think about this scenario for my demonstration? I start with a quick history of cigars, how they were invented in Cuba by the Taino people, the arrival of Christopher Columbus and how his sailors took *seegars*, as the locals called them, back to Spain. Then I do a short bit about how cigars are rolled by hand." From the bag he plucked a handful of pictures. "I've got photos showing the entire process."

"Very enlightening."

"I'll explain how the cigar band came into the picture. And then I'll present a how-to demonstration. You know, trimming, lighting, and so forth."

"This entire production is unnecessary, you know."

"Gotta keep to the plan, Professor. After I show the proper way to trim and light, I thought I'd do an audience-participation thing by bringing someone forward to give it a try. That's why I brought cutters. I'll hand them out with cigars and let everyone try trimming them. What do you think of the show?"

"It certainly seems comprehensive."

"I think so. Now what say you to a drink? By my reckoning, it's the cocktail hour."

When they entered the parlor, Bill Restivo's only customer at the bar was Harry Hardin.

"Thank God you're here," he exclaimed, turning toward

them. "I was afraid I'd be drinking all alone." He turned to Restivo. "My good man, arm these gentlemen with their heart's desire."

Nick asked for a Jameson's. Woolley ordered scotch.

"May I offer a toast on this night of beastly weather?" said Harry. "In the words of the Immortal Bard in *King Lear*, ' 'Tis a naughty night to swim in.' " He sipped his drink and winked. "But, ah, what a night for . . . a *murder!*"

Presently the others drifted into the parlor.

Sheila Stevens was first, giving Harry a kiss on the cheek and ordering a vodka martini.

Simon Cane came next. Saying nothing and choosing not to drink, he sat in a chair facing a window with an expression on his face as dark as the view.

Nigel Wilson and Clifford Branson entered laughing and greeted everyone in the room with nods, then carried drinks to facing leather armchairs beneath Natalie's portrait.

A few moments later, Richard Edwards and Parker Slade reprised their arrival of the previous evening.

Felicity Dane entered with Ivo Bogdanovich, each carrying a tray of Nora Swanson's delicious appetizers.

"Now with bated breath, according to the stage directions," said Harry, "the cast awaits the grand entrance of the lady who signs all their checks."

Tony Biciano entered alone and went to the bar.

"Nice touch. Pure Hitchcock," said Harry, leading Sheila away from the bar. "Definitely heightens tension."

Holding a glass of bourbon in his left hand, Tony placed the right on Nick's shoulder and said, "I wish you could have joined us for the fishing."

Nick smiled. "I had a report that I was the subject of quite a discussion."

Tony held up the glass as if to make a toast. "It's a Hollywood rule. The person who's not at the party gets talked about."

"Where's Natalie?"

"She's working in her office."

"Are you sure?"

"She left a note for me on her door saying she doesn't want to be disturbed and she'll be joining us for dinner."

Nick put down his glass. "Excuse me, but I'll feel better when I see her myself."

Woolley exclaimed, "I'll go with you."

"Relax, fellas," Tony said. "Since everyone is here, what could possibly happen?"

Finding the note, Nick pressed an ear to the door, heard nothing within, rapped hard, and shouted, "Natalie? It's Nick."

A moment later he heard the click of a lock. The door swung open, and Natalie greeted him with a quizzical smile.

"Just checking," said Nick.

She touched him lightly on his left cheek. "How very sweet." She looked at Woolley. "Of both of you. But with the door locked and no access to this room from windows, you may rest assured that I'm perfectly safe. I have been all day."

"That's because between Woolley and me your guests were being watched. I assumed that when the boat returned, Tony would be with you."

"As indeed he has been until a few minutes ago. I have just a few odds and ends to clear up. Then I'll join you all for dinner."

"Until then I want Woolley either in your office or outside the door, or you can leave the odds and ends and come with us."

She thought a moment. "Very well, the odds and ends can wait."

Flanked by Nick and Woolley, she entered the parlor exclaiming, "I am so sorry about this rambunctious weather."

Everyone in the room turned.

"It was not in the forecast for this weekend," she said, moving to the bar. "Still, it contributes an atmosphere of suspense, don't you all agree?"

Woolley replied, "Harry believes you ordered it from the special effects department."

"How cute and clever of Harry," said Natalie, smiling at him.

"The idea of storm effects being created to establish a mood of suspense for a gathering such as this," Harry said, "was in fact done in a charming film titled *Murder by Death*."

"As I recall, it was Neil Simon's delicious send-up of detective stories with characters who were caricatures of the classic fictional sleuths—Sam Spade, Charlie Chan, Nick Charles, Poirot, and, of course, Miss Marple. They were invited to dinner by a man named Lionel Twain, played by Truman Capote, of all people. Am I right?"

"Twain challenged them to solve a murder that had not been committed—his own—but would be by midnight."

"Wouldn't it be wonderful if all screenwriters were as inventive as Neil Simon? Or even half?" To Restivo she said, "A snifter of my cognac, please, Bill."

"How nice to see you, Natalie," said Sheila Stevens from across the room. "How was your day?"

"Frightfully busy," she said, taking the glass from Restivo. Looking around the room, she found Felicity Dane and called out to her, "Darling, please go to the kitchen and tell Nora that I'd like her to serve dinner now."

Felicity handed a tray to Ivo and hurried from the room.

Natalie sipped the cognac. "I'm sure everyone who went fishing today must be terribly hungry by now. My third husband always came back from fishing feeling ravenous."

As dinner was eaten, Nick found the tension around the table almost palpable. Nora's sumptuous feast of lobster bisque, a fish course of delicately seasoned scrod, perfectly broiled lamb chops, baked potatoes, steamed broccoli, a salad of crisp lettuce, and appropriate wines was barely touched. But in view of what had transpired the previous evening in the form of Natalie's How would each of you murder me? game, he appreciated why no one but Woolley, Tony, and Natalie exhibited an appetite. The conversation was desultory and limited to the subject of the motion picture business—the grosses of films in release, deals being made for future films, films in development, films in preproduction, films in progress, films so bad they were going straight to home video.

Through all of this, Natalie appeared to be listening attentively. While adding nothing to the exchanges of opinion, she was a presence that could not be ignored. The elephant in a corner. A silent potentate presiding over her courtiers and courtesans, weighing the value of each. And, perhaps, deciding whose head should be chopped off for the greater good of a realm built on a flaw in the human eye that allowed a series of still pictures of people, animals, and objects arranged in a rapidly flowing sequence on a strand of celluloid and projected on a screen appear to be moving.

With dinner over, Natalie announced, "Coffee and after-dinner drinks will be served in the parlor, where we are going to be treated to an informal talk by Nick Chase on the fascinating topic that is so dear to his heart and so much a part of our film—cigars."

Twenty-seven

WHILE DINNER WAS in progress, Ivo Bogdanovich and Bill Restivo had rearranged furniture in the parlor. Armchairs that had been scattered around the large room were now grouped in the center, backs toward the bar and facing a small table set up for Nick's talk.

When Nick came in, Ivo asked, "Will this setup do?"

"It's just fine," Nick said. "Now may I impose on you to accompany me to my room to help me bring the things I'll be needing?"

"Maybe after your talk I'll try smoking a cigar," said Ivo as they left the parlor. "I might find out that I like it."

"There's nothing that pleases a man who sells cigars more than winning a convert."

As they walked along the corridor to Nick's room, Ivo said, "Can I ask you something, Nick? It's not about cigars."

"Fire away."

"Everybody seems to think that somebody's trying to kill Natalie—"

"Apparently so."

"And that you're here to find out who. Is it true? Not that someone's trying to kill her, because someone obviously is, what with that shot being fired at her and that light nearly falling on her. But is it true that it could be someone in this house and you're here to find out who?"

Nick opened the door to his room. "May I ask you a question?"

"Absolutely."

Nick stepped aside to let Ivo enter the room, followed him in, and closed the door.

"You know Natalie's guests pretty well, right?"

"I guess so."

"Which of them do you think would be capable of trying to kill her? Not which one might like to see Natalie dead, but which of them, in your estimation, would have the guts to actually attempt to commit murder?"

"You're really putting me on the spot."

"I sure am."

"Maybe this is because he's a money man and I don't like bean counters, but I wouldn't put it past Mr. Wilson."

"Can you explain why?"

"He's a sneaky bastard."

"Sneaky!"

"Yeah. He was always asking me about why something's being done this way, why three guys are doing something that he figures two could handle, and stuff like that. I tried to explain to him that the motion picture business is highly unionized. But I get the impression that Wilson suspected Natalie of trying to put something over on him. I finally got fed up with it and told him if he thought something was fishy he should take it up with the unit manager. He's the one who keeps track of a picture's budget on a day by day basis."

Nick collected the items he needed for his talk. "Who's unit manager on this picture?"

"When we started, it was a woman named Cindy Raphael," said Ivo as Nick handed him cigar boxes, "but Natalie replaced her and turned the job over to Tony Biciano."

"Do you know if Wilson talked to Tony?"

"He must have, because a few days later, when we were having preproduction meetings at Natalie's ranch, I was passing her office and overheard Natalie and Tony arguing with him."

"Were you able to make out what they were saying?"

"It was a row about the film being already way over budget. Wilson was demanding that Natalie replace Tony as unit manager and bring in an accountant from Simon Cane's firm."

"Did you hear Natalie's response?"

"She said the only way Tony would be replaced was over her dead body."

"Thanks, Ivo. I'm sorry for putting you on the spot."

"As long as I'm on it," Ivo said as they left the room, "I might as well name my second nominee for somebody you should keep an eye on, and that's Rich Edwards."

"Why him?"

"This may sound weird, but I happen to know that Rich, who is gay, in case you didn't know, got really pissed off at Natalie because she took Tony Biciano away from him. He went on a two-week bender. Rich has a drinking problem. Anyway, I figure that Rich might be thinking that if he got Natalie out of the way, he'd not only take over running New Millennium Films, he'd get Tony back."

"Where would that leave Parker Slade?"

Ivo chuckled. "You have been observant."

"The relationship is hard to miss."

"The thing between Rich and Parker is strictly physical," Ivo said as they approached the door to the parlor. "Rich was in love with Tony. He still is."

While Ivo and Nick placed the items for Nick's talk on the small table, the audience was clustered around the bar and seemed to be having a good time. Perhaps this was because of the drinks being served by Bill Restivo, Nick thought, or maybe the congenial atmosphere had been imposed by a realization that they were on an island in the midst of a howling storm. Or might they be relishing the notion that each of them was considered by their hostess and boss as a suspect in a plot to murder her? The only thing Nick was sure of as Natalie downed her drink, left the bar, and crossed the room to the small table was that it was unlikely any of them would be in the least interested in listening to him talk about cigars.

Looking at the items on the table, Natalie asked, "Are you ready, Nick?"

"You know, Natalie, I really don't have to go on with this."

"Of course you do, my dear. Everyone would be so disappointed if you didn't." With that, she turned and clapped her hands loudly. "Attention, everyone! Nick is ready to begin his talk!" Leaving him, she returned to the bar. "Take your drinks with you and find chairs. You, too, Bill. As of now the bar is closed. And you, Felicity. There'll be no eating, either. I shall expect each of you to give Nick your undivided attention."

Nick waited while they took seats.

Carrying a drink to a chair at the rear of the grouping, Harry Hardin asked, "Will there be a quiz after you talk, Nick?"

"If there is," said Tony Biciano, a glass of port in hand as he sat to Harry's right, "I hope it will be multiple choice. I'm not good at writing essays."

Sheila Stevens carried a flute of champagne and sat at Harry's left. In a row in front of her, Harry, and Tony were Cane, Wilson, and Branson. Before them, Edwards and Slade sat side by side. Standing against a wall to Nick's left were Bogdanovic and Restivo. Looking like a chaperone at a school dance whose job was to ensure no one spiked the punch, Natalie was behind the bar, holding but not drinking a snifter of her prized cognac. Felicity sat to her left. In order to lend moral support to Nick, Woolley chose a large armchair closest to him.

After offering Woolley a quick, reassuring smile, Nick swallowed hard, held up a cigar, and said, "Chances are your father celebrated your birth by handing out a bunch of these."

The talk went as planned. A brief history of cigars. Invented in Cuba. Columbus and his crew taking *seegars* back to Spain. How cigars are hand-rolled—pictures of the process circulated among the audience. The cigar band applied first to keep the wrappers from coming loose, then as a trademark. Explaining that the color of the wrapper, the length, and the thickness (known as the ring gauge), determined strength and flavor. The way to trim, light, and smoke a cigar.

Going around the room, he passed out cigars, clippers, and boxes of matches.

As he handed a clipper to Tony Biciano, Tony said, "I see what you're up to, Nick. This is your sneaky way of getting our fingerprints."

Laughing at his joke, he jabbed an elbow against Harry Hardin's arm, causing Harry's drink to spill.

"You idiot," Harry exclaimed, bolting from his chair and brushing off the liquor. "What do I do for a drink now? The damned bar's closed."

With a witheringly rebuking look at Tony, Natalie left the bar and handed Harry her glass of cognac. "Take mine. I haven't touched it."

Felicity arrived to give Harry a napkin and to take away the glass that had been spilled. She looked at Natalie. "Shall I bring you another cognac, or do you prefer to pour one yourself?"

"I'm just fine," Natalie said sharply. "Go to the kitchen and bring us fresh coffee."

"Yes, ma'am," she said, hurrying away.

Tony said to Nick, "I'm sorry I interrupted your show."

"No harm done. I was finished."

"And a great show it was," declared Harry. Lifting his new drink, he looked around the room and said, "Folks, I propose a toast. To Nick Chase! Master of cigars . . . master detective."

He drank the cognac in a single gulp.

Clutching his throat, he muttered, "What the hell—"

The snifter slipped from his hand.

Gasping for breath, he collapsed into his chair and breathed a long, agonized sigh.

Nick bent over him, searched for a pulse in the right carotid artery, then the left, and found none. Straightening, he said, "He's dead." Retrieving the fallen brandy glass, he sniffed it twice. "Most likely cyanide."

"Oh, my god," Natalie cried. "That was *my drink.*"

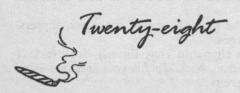

Twenty-eight

WITH WOOLLEY DISPATCHED to Natalie's office to telephone the police in Portsmouth, Nick addressed the stunned
and horrified guests in the parlor. "Until the police get here,
this room is off limits. Can the door be locked, Natalie?"

"Yes. The key is in my office." She turned to Tony Biciano. "You know where it is."

Tony left to fetch it.

"Everything is to be left as is," Nick said, "including the
body."

Sheila sobbed, "Can you . . . cover it . . . him . . . with
something?"

Nick turned to Natalie. "A bedsheet will do."

"Yes, of course," she said. "Felicity, bring one right
away."

"Yes, ma'am."

"Be sure it's a clean one," Nick said.

Felicity gave a nod and left the room.

Nick addressed the group. "For now I think it's best that
you all go to your rooms. The police will want to talk to
each of you, probably in the morning."

Wordless and grim-faced, they filed from the room.

Tony returned with the key. "Is there anything I can do,
Nick?"

Nick took the key. "No. This is a police matter now."

Leaving the room, Tony paused in the doorway. "That poison *was* meant for Natalie. If I find out who put it in her drink—"

"This is a *police* matter, Tony."

As Tony left, Felicity came with the sheet, and Nick covered the body. When she was gone, he went behind the bar.

Woolley returned. "I've spoken to a Lieutenant Fran Schneidau of the Portsmouth Police Department."

"What did he have to say?"

"*Fran* is a woman."

"Hooray for the Portsmouth police! When will she be here?"

"That depends entirely on the weather. There are small craft warnings posted all the way from Marblehead, Massachusetts, to Bar Harbor, Maine. Schneidau hopes to be here around the middle of tomorrow morning, conditions permitting. In the meantime, she asks that we do our best to preserve the crime scene. I informed her that there is a former New York City homicide detective on the premises. I also told her that in all likelihood when she gets here the perpetrator of this murder will be in custody."

Nick bent and sniffed the open top of the cognac bottle.

Woolley asked, "Anything?"

Nick shook his head. "The cyanide was added to the cognac in the snifter."

"What a dastardly thing." He gazed at the body. "And what bad luck for Harry. But now we know that Natalie was right in believing one of the people in this house wants to kill her."

"There's a large field of suspects, that's for sure."

"Will you have a favorite to recommend to Lieutenant Schneidau?"

"I've no doubt that she's capable of doing her own handicapping. I wish her luck."

"You're not stepping aside?"

"Oh, yes I am," Nick said, coming from behind the bar. "I'll tell Schneidau what I know, which isn't much, catch the first flight to Boston, and then a cab to Cambridge." He paused by the sheet-draped body. "For all the good I did, I could have stayed there."

"I am very, very sorry," said Clifford Branson as he walked Sheila Stevens to her room. "I know how deeply you and Harry were in love."

She brushed away a tear and forced a smile. "Best lay I ever had."

"That line might play for a Joan Crawford or a Kathleen Turner, doll, but this is Cliffie you're talking to."

"You always were a script doctor." She gulped breath. "What a field day the tabloid TV shows are going to have with this story! Action-movie superstar Harry Hardin murdered! It will be an orgy of old film clips. Harry barechested in *Operation Rescue.* Harry's nude love scene in *Deep Space Ten.* In a month or so we'll have the inevitable "The True Hollywood Story" on the E! cable network about the mysterious death of Harry Hardin. Then, maybe in a year or so, a two-night, four-hour miniseries bio-pic produced by New Millennium Films, full of talking heads claiming they were Harry's friends and—"

As she choked with grief, Cliff enveloped her in his arms. "Go ahead, kid, cry your heart out."

Regaining her composure, Sheila said, "That damned poisoned drink was meant for that lousy bitch Natalie!"

Richard Edwards entered his room and went straight to the bedside telephone. "What a movie this night would make," he said, puffing a cigarette as he punched a Los Angeles area code on the number pad.

Parker Slade sat beside him on the bed. "Who are you calling?"

Rich grinned. "Sid Goldstein in publicity. This story has got to come out with our spin."

Parker pinched Rich's bicep. "Do you know what you are? A whore, that's what. A slut."

"Honey, this is the sweetest thing that's ever happened to me. And to you."

Goldstein answered sleepily.

"Sid? It's Rich. Hold onto something, 'cause this is gonna rock you like an earthquake."

Nigel Wilson and Simon Cane conversed in the dining room.

"You're the legal eagle of this outfit," Nigel said excitedly. "What's New Millennium's liability in this disaster?"

"None whatsoever. Harry Hardin's death will be recorded as an accident. Whoever put poison in that cognac wasn't trying to kill *him*. That lethal stuff was meant for Natalie. If Harry's estate looks for grounds to sue anybody, it will have to be a case of wrongful death against the person who poisoned Natalie's drink."

"The police will know that it had to be one of us."

"In my opinion this was so cleverly done that they'll never find out who did it."

"What about Nick Chase?"

"The man was too busy fiddling around with his cigars to notice anything."

"Perhaps, but I'd feel better if Natalie hadn't brought him here."

Wringing hands and pacing the small room shared with Ivo Bogdanovich, Bill Restivo said, "I know the police are going to question me about how it was possible for someone to put poison in that cognac bottle. They may think I did it."

Ivo was lying on his bed. "That's baloney. That bottle has been on the bar since last night. Anybody could've come in at any time and dropped in a little arsenic."

"Nick said it was cyanide."

Ivo listened to the howling wind. "I hate storms."

"I hate the idea of the police questioning me."

"They have to question everyone. I'm kind of looking forward to it."

"Well, I'm not."

"If anybody's going to figure out what happened, I'm betting my dough on Nick."

Bill sat on his bed. "How much?"

Ivo sat up.

"You want to bet on who solves this murder?"

"You brought up the subject of betting."

"Okay. I'll back Nick solving it to the tune of twenty bucks."

"You're on."

They shook hands.

"Right," said Ivo, lying back. "Now, who do you think slipped the stuff into that bottle?"

"I haven't the foggiest idea."

"It could have been Tony Biciano."

"Why would Tony kill the woman who's supporting him?"

"I figure he's got to be in Natalie's will for a bundle of dough, if for no other reason than Natalie's gratitude for all the pounding he's been giving her."

"You have a very dirty mind."

Ivo laughed. "Ain't I awful?"

"How goes it with Felicity?"

"Now who's got the dirty mind?"

"She looked awfully shook up. I think you should be comforting her."

"If you can find a way to get Nora out of their room, I'd be glad to."

The cook had learned what happened in the parlor from Felicity. On her way to find the clean sheet she had burst into the kitchen.

"Oh Nora, something horrible happened."

Nora looked up from a pot she'd been scrubbing.

"What did you drop and break now?"

Felicity raised a hand to her neck. "One of the guests choked to death. Somebody put some poison in a drink."

"How terrible. Who would do such a thing?"

Felicity shrugged. "Someone very clever."

Accompanied to her room by Tony, Natalie had gone straight to bed.

"What a night," she said wearily. "I'm afraid I'm too much on edge to sleep."

Tony settled beside her. "I'm pretty tense myself."

Natalie listened to wind-driven rain pelting the windows. "How long do you think it will be until the police will be able to get out here?"

"My guess is they probably won't try till daylight."

"Which is when?"

"The sun will be up around six o'clock."

She sighed deeply. "I'll be glad when this is over."

Woolley had taken up what had become to Nick a familiar stance at the window of Nick's room. "What with the rain and the fog," he said, peering into the blackness beyond, "I can't see a thing. I don't imagine the police will be rushing out to brave this storm."

"There's no reason they should," said Nick from a closet where he was hanging up his shirt. "No one's going to be leaving this island anytime soon."

He came out of the closet in pajamas Kevin and Noreen had given to him on a birthday. He looked at Woolley affectionately.

"What was it Harry Hardin said? ' 'Tis a naughty night to swim in.' "

"What a tragic loss," Woolley said.

He left the window and sat in a chair.

"Such a good actor."

"If you say so."

"I do. I believe he would have made a fine Hamlet."

"A bit long in the tooth for the melancholy Dane, I think."

"Many older men have played the role convincingly. Richard Burton for instance."

"I still say Harry Hardin was much too young to have been cast as me."

"I wonder whom Natalie will select to take over for him?"

"I'm sure she'll find someone."

"I suppose they will have to redo all the scenes they shot at your store."

Nick groaned. "If they do, my neighbors on Brattle Street will string me up."

PART VIII

Dirty Laundry

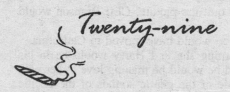

Twenty-nine

AT SIX IN the morning Nora shook Felicity hard. "Come on, girl, get up."

Felicity opened her eyes, yawned, and pulled the sheet to her neck. "Go away and leave me be. I'm tired."

Nora yanked off the sheet. "There's work to be done. There may be a dead man in the house, but everyone's going to be wanting breakfast. And lunch. And then cocktails. And then dinner. Get moving, girl."

Sitting up, Felicity thought for a moment about last night.

"Someday, when I'm rich," she said, getting out of bed, "I'll be able to stay in bed until noon. Maybe even later."

"You'll never get rich being a maid."

"I've been observing Mrs. Goodman and her guests. Why shouldn't I live like them?"

"Well, someday is someday. Right now you've got work to do. Go and get Ivo and Bill out of bed and the three of you set up the table in the dining room. There's no telling when the guests will be up and about, but one thing is for sure, they're going to want lots of coffee and juice and something to eat."

Wide awake and all cried out, Sheila Stevens had spent a night of relentless wind and rain pondering what might have been.

If she hadn't fought with Natalie about changes Natalie wanted in the script of *Smoking Out a Killer*, this weekend would not have happened.

If she had simply quit the picture, Cliff Branson would have taken over.

Then the production would have moved to California.

On a Sunday morning she and Harry would be in his house in Malibu, and he would be making love to her with the background music of the gentle sounds of the Pacific Ocean.

If Tony hadn't been so clumsy, there would have been no spilled drink.

If she could have prevented Natalie from giving Harry the glass of cognac, Harry would be alive and Natalie would be dead.

She suddenly thought of Cliff Branson and how sweet he was in showing concern for her.

The night had passed for Cliff in a series of dreams. Probably because he was a writer, he usually had them in a linear manner. Like movies, they had a beginning, middle, and end, but he rarely remembered them. However, he vividly recalled the one that had jolted him awake.

Nick Chase had stormed into his room, waving around a cigar and bellowing, "All right, Cliff, it's time for you to confess. Why did you kill Natalie?"

"But I didn't."

"Don't argue with me. I'm a detective."

Simon Cane had been awake all night listening to the storm and brooding.

Now he gazed from his window at weather that showed no signs of letting up anytime soon. Until the storm broke and the ocean calmed, there was no getting off the island.

By now, he'd hoped, he would have been on his way back to New York.

As Harry Hardin's attorney and agent he confronted the daunting task of settling the legal and practical affairs that would now flow from his death.

A statement would have to be written and released. What to say?

It is with deep regret and sorrow that I announce the untimely death of a truly great star. . . .

How to handle explaining the cause?

He died of poisoning when he drank a glass of cognac intended for someone else.

In addition to returning to New York to dispose of the case of Wieser vs. Morris, he now would have to deal with the police concerning release of the body.

Then he would have to arrange to get it back to California.

A funeral must be planned.

How to handle the vultures in the press that would quickly circle the corpse in search of tasty morsels about how and why he'd died?

Harry's last will and testament must be probated.

Insurance policies needed to be dealt with.

When a movie superstar dies, he thought, as he looked forlornly at the implacable storm, there are ongoing repercussions and ramifications. Residuals. Contracts to be settled.

There would be licensing of the Harry Hardin image and name. Posters, T-shirts, and all the other collectibles in a bizarre world in which a dead star goes on making millions of dollars. If Marilyn Monroe, James Dean, John Wayne, W. C. Fields, Charlie Chaplin, Oliver and Hardy, and even The Three Stooges and others were any measure, prospects for profits were enormous.

But there was another client to attend—Natalie Goodman's New Millennium Films.

What would Harry's death mean for *Smoking Out a Killer*?

Cancellation of production? Delay and regrouping?

In talking with Nigel Wilson in the dining room after Nick Chase had told them all to go to their rooms, Nigel had urged that the film be shelved.

He had told Nigel it was worth considering.

But in all these pressing matters, until he could find some way to escape Pirate's Cove, his hands were tied.

When Nigel decided at half-past three in the morning that it was useless to try to sleep, he got out of bed and launched another review of the deplorable condition of the film's finances. To continue production was certainly possible.

But was that a wise course?

A better one would be to scrap the film. The industry would understand. To scuttle the film was a rational decision and in strict accordance with sound business practices.

Having had a short but restful night's sleep, Richard Edwards awoke to the dark-brown aftertaste of one of Nick Chase's cigars.

After awakening Sid Goldstein with the news of Harry's death, he'd smoked the cigar while he and Parker Slade were in bed talking about what happened at the conclusion of Nick's surprisingly engaging talk.

"When Harry gulped down Natalie's drink and started making that awful choking noise," Parker had said as he got out of his clothes, "I thought he was joking around. I've never seen a dead body, let alone seeing somebody croak right before my eyes."

"I thought Harry handled the scene very well," Rich said, drawing on the cigar.

Parker got onto the bed. "What's going to happen now with the film?"

Rich blew a column of smoke and placed the half-smoked cigar into an ashtray. "That's entirely up to Natalie."

Parker snuggled against Rich's back and sighed. "What do we do now?"

"We wait. We bide our time. What happened doesn't change anything. I know exactly what I'm doing. Now how about a kiss? "

When Parker drew away, he'd said, "You taste of tobacco. But it's kind of nice."

Further talk of Harry's death and what it might mean to

them had been abandoned, and after a while, exhausted and spent, they had drifted asleep in each other's arms.

A few hours later, as Rich left the bed and went into the bathroom to rinse away the dark-brown taste, he felt amazingly relaxed.

At a quarter past seven, as Nick dressed, the knock on the door, he presumed, would be Professor Woolley.

"Come in!"

Tony Biciano entered. "Excuse me, Nick, but there's a phone call for you on Natalie's private line in her office. It's a Lieutenant Schneidau."

"I don't suppose the call can be switched to my phone."

"No, I'm sorry."

As they left the room, Nick asked, "How is Natalie holding up?"

"Very well, considering the close call she had."

"Yes, indeed."

When they reached the office Tony said, "Your call's on line two, the one that's lit up."

"Thank you."

Nick punched the button and picked up the receiver. "Nick Chase here."

"It's Lieutenant Fran Schneidau. I'm afraid it's going to be hours before I can get out to Pirate's Cove. I'm trying to line up a Coast Guard cutter. But they've got their hands full in this gale, as you can imagine. Even if I can grab one, it's likely to be quite a while before I can get a crime scene team out there. I understand from Mr. Woolley that you're a retired homicide cop."

"Emphasis on retired."

"That's not what I heard from Mr. Woolley."

"The man's a mystery writer. He has a vivid imagination."

"I thought it would be helpful to me if you could brief me, so that when I get out there, I'll be up to speed on just what happened last night."

"I'd be glad to, Lieutenant."

"Call me Fran."

"And I'm Nick."

"So fill me in."

"It's a long story."

"They usually are. Take your time."

He quickly related the circumstances of Woolley's relationship with Natalie Goodman and his novel being made into a movie by Natalie's company. Natalie's tale of the van trying to run her car off a freeway. The bullet hole in the window of her Santa Barbara house. The falling light. The remarkable dinner at Farley's. The shot at Natalie there and as she returned to the Copley Plaza. The voyage on the yacht. Possible motives. Natalie's list of suspects. How Harry Hardin drank a poisoned cognac intended for Natalie.

"Well, that's one good thing about this weather," said Schneidau. "We won't have to go looking for suspects. You've got 'em all there. And I'm lucky to have you there with them. The whole process can be speeded up if you'd agree to take initial statements. Okay with you?"

"If you think I can be useful—"

The door flew open, and Ivo Bogdanovich burst into the office. Breathless, he blurted. "Nick, you gotta come. You're not gonna believe this. There's been another murder."

"Who? Is it Natalie?"

Ivo gulped air. "No. It's Felicity."

Schneidau asked urgently, "Nick, what is it?"

"It seems there's been another murder."

"What the hell's going on out there?"

"I'll get back to you." He hung up the phone. "Okay, Ivo, where's the body?"

"She's in the laundry room. It's in the basement. Nora found her."

Thirty

"IT'S MY UNDERSTANDING," said Ivo as he led Nick toward a stairway, "that the laundry room was built in what used to be part of an old missile base."

When Nick descended stairs to the basement, he found Nora and Bill Restivo just outside the laundry room. She looked composed, almost serene, but Nick recognized that it was shock. When he looked at her closely, she began speaking as if she were in a trance.

"I don't know what got into that girl today. Ever since I woke her, she was nothing but surly to me. She was supposed to be setting up for breakfast, but when I went looking for her, she wasn't there, just Ivo and Bill."

"That's right," Ivo said. "She'd been acting strange, very nervous, and then all of a sudden she just up and went."

Nora said, "I came down here to the laundry room to get napkins from the dryer. When I saw her I went and got the boys."

Nick stepped past her and looked into the laundry room.

Parallel to a washing machine and a dryer and in the middle of a wide, almost perfectly circular pool of blood, Felicity lay on her left side. The gaping slit in her throat formed a loop from just below the right ear to the corner of the left jaw.

"Thank you, Nora. I think you'd better lie down for a

while," said Nick. "Bill, take her to her room. And then I want you to stand at the top of the stairway and keep anyone from coming down here."

As they were leaving, Natalie and Tony appeared at the door.

Natalie looked at the body, recoiled against Tony, and gasped. "Oh, my lord!"

Nick exclaimed angrily, "Tony, get her the hell out of here."

When they were gone, he took two steps into the room and found a footprint in the blood. He knelt to examine it. "Ivo, has anybody been in here since Nora found her?"

"That's my footprint, Nick. I went in that far to see if she was alive."

"Did you touch her?"

"Hell, no. I could tell with one look that she had to be dead."

Nick rose and backed out of the room. "Off hand, I'd say she died instantly."

"Thank god. I mean thank god she didn't suffer. But who'd want to kill a maid?"

"The same person who killed Harry Hardin, of course. I think the odds are astronomically against there being two killers on this cursed island."

"Man, I thought stuff like this only happened in movies. Look at that poor kid. She was pretty enough to be in pictures."

"As I recall, she said she wanted to be in the hotel business or maybe a cruise director."

Woolley's voice boomed down the stairs. "Young man, I insist you let me pass."

Nick shouted, "It's all right, Bill. Let him down. He's an ally."

Thumping tread and voice preceded him. " Nick, this is awful. Just awful."

When he reached Nick, he peered into the room. "Ghastly. Poor thing."

"I'd say she was standing with her back to the open door. She was grabbed by the hair. With the head pulled back, the knife was plunged into the right side of her neck and drawn to the left. No time to struggle. No way to scream."

Woolley stroked his beard. "I agree."

"There's nothing more to see or do here," Nick said.

Ivo reached for the door.

"Leave it as is, Ivo," Nick said. "Lieutenant Schneidau's criminalists will be very upset if we mess around with their crime scene."

Woolley grunted. "If they ever manage to get here."

Ascending the stairs, Nick said, "Well, Professor, what would Jake Elwell make of this second murder?"

"Jake would deduce, as have you, that the unfortunate girl in the laundry room was somehow involved in the event of last night, probably as an accomplice to whoever has set his sights on murdering Natalie. This girl could easily have put the cyanide into Natalie's cognac."

"That is within the realm of the possible," said Nick as they reached the top of the stairs, "or she could have seen who did."

Bill Restivo asked, "How long do you want me to stand guard here, Nick?"

"I think it's safe to abandon the gate, Bill. It's unlikely that this will be an instance of the criminal returning to the scene of the crime."

Except for Natalie, Tony, and Sheila Stevens, the guests were assembled in the dining room. The buffet-style breakfast of scrambled eggs, bacon and sausages, potatoes, toast, and an assortment of fruit was hardly touched, although a table littered with cups and saucers suggested a great deal of coffee had been consumed. Despite a glowing chandelier and the light from wall sconces, the room seemed overwhelmed by the bleakness of weather beyond the windows and the knowledge that another murder had been committed. Widely spaced around the table, the five figures appeared both dispirited and wary.

As Woolley, Ivo, and Bill went directly to the buffet, five pairs of eyes that had scrupulously avoided contact with each other turned expectantly toward Nick.

He stood where Natalie had presided over two dinners. "I'm sure you all have heard that the maid, Felicity Dane, has been found dead in the laundry room. Obviously, each of you must be considered a suspect in her murder and in the death of Harry Hardin. I've spoken by phone to Lieutenant Schneidau of the Portsmouth Police Department. She and her associates will be here as soon as possible. Given the state of the weather, she has no idea when that will be. However, in the meantime she's asked me to act in her stead by taking statements from each of you. You have the right to refuse to speak to me, of course. But I believe it will speed up the process and allow you to get out of here as quickly as possible. Except, of course, for the murderer. If you choose to cooperate, I'll be available in my room in ten minutes. I'll leave it to you to decide among yourselves what order in which you come."

Before leaving them to consider his proposition, Nick went to the breakfast buffet and said to Woolley, "Fix me up a plate of whatever you're having, please, and bring it and yourself up to my room. I'll need your assistance in this."

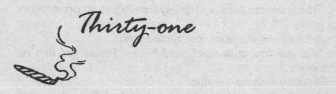

Thirty-one

W:HEN WOOLLEY ENTERED Nick's room with Nick's breakfast on a tray, Nick was seated in an armchair by the window and hanging up the phone.

"I've just reported to Lieutenant Schneidau. She accepts my opinion that we have a single murder case with two victims, the second of whom was not part of the killer's original plan."

Woolley placed the heavy tray on the bureau. "Did she say when she expects to be able to join us?"

"The Coast Guard commander in Portsmouth, or wherever he is, is working on freeing up a boat. They are a little swamped, no joke intended."

Woolley went to the window. "Blast this storm!"

Nick investigated his breakfast. "Don't be so quick to wish it away. At the moment the elements are on our side. There's nothing like a feeling of claustrophobia in getting a suspect to crack. That's why the interview rooms in police stations are always small. They're designed to make a guilty man feel the walls are closing in on him. I wish we had a lie-detector machine."

"Very unreliable devices, as well you know."

Nick scooped scrambled eggs onto toast. "Yes, but they're invaluable in shaking a man's confidence. I've found the mere mention of hooking up a lie detector to a guilty man is likely to prompt a confession."

Woolley helped himself to a strip of crisp bacon. "And if a man is innocent?"

"The innocent man will always welcome an opportunity to prove it."

A knock on the door interrupted them.

"Ah, our first customer," said Nick. "Please see him in, Professor."

Woolley opened the door.

Simon Cane blurted, "Why are you here?"

"Come in, Counselor," said Nick. "I've asked Professor Woolley to take notes. And for your protection, he's also a witness."

"Very well, but make this quick. I have a number of telephone calls to make."

"Please take the chair by the window. As a matter of personal curiosity, would you mind telling me how you came to be first?"

"We drew lots. I lost."

"I'll try not to keep you long."

"I'll tell you straight away that I had nothing to do with the death of Harry Hardin or the maid. I was in the dining room when she died."

"What time was that?"

"By my reckoning she has to have been killed only a few minutes before you came in and started ordering us around."

"How do you come to that conclusion? She might have been dead for quite some time before her body was discovered."

"That's not possible."

"Why not?"

"I saw her in the corridor as I was on my way into breakfast. I glimpsed her going toward Natalie's suite, carrying a tray. Natalie's breakfast, I presume. Or Tony's."

"Did you speak to her?"

"I had no reason to."

"How did she seem to you?"

"In what respect?"

"Was she pleasant? Rude? Did she appear nervous?"

"I really wasn't close enough to her to notice her mood."

"Would you agree with me that the drink that killed Harry was meant to kill Natalie?"

"It would seem so."

"Has Natalie informed you that there have been other attempts on her life?"

"I heard on the news that a shot had been fired at her in Boston, but I was on my way to LaGuardia Airport at the time and was unable to speak to her to confirm it."

"Did she tell you about an attempt to run her car off a freeway in Los Angeles and a shot that was fired into her house in Santa Barbara?"

"First I've heard of either."

"Really? You were in L.A. at the time of the Santa Barbara incident."

"Be that as it may, I knew nothing about it."

"Has Natalie expressed a concern about you representing both her and Harry Hardin?"

"I fail to see why that arrangement should interest you."

"Are you a drinking man, Mr. Cane?"

"I enjoy a drink before dinner."

"What do you drink?"

"Scotch."

"Is that what you were drinking last night?"

"As I recall, I had one before dinner and another after."

"Can you suggest why anyone would want to kill Natalie?"

"I can think of several reasons, actually. Natalie makes enemies easily. That's why she is such a success in an industry renowned for its buccaneers and other cutthroats. One does not make movies, sir, without stepping on toes, kicking asses, and otherwise bruising egos."

"Who would benefit financially or in other ways from her death?"

"I am Natalie's attorney, and that is privileged information."

"Yes, of course. Thanks for your cooperation, sir."

"That's it?"

"There is one more thing. On the table beside you there's a notepad and pen. I'd like you to print your name on it."

"Whatever for?"

Nick smiled. "Humor me."

Cane scooped up the pad, grabbed the pen, and printed his name. "Now is that it?"

"Yes. Thank you."

When the door closed behind Cane, Nick picked up the notepad, tore off the top sheet, and slipped it into a pocket.

"Your purpose in having him print his name, I take it," Woolley said, "is to compare it with the note that Natalie received."

Before Nick could answer, there was a knock on the door.

"Come in, please," Nick called.

Nigel Wilson entered.

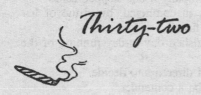

Thirty-two

"PLEASE TAKE THE chair by the window, Mr. Wilson," said Nick, standing by the bureau. "Would you care for a cup of coffee?"

Wilson sat. "No, thank you. I generally have one cup a day, and I've had it."

"I drink too much of it. I've asked Professor Woolley to take notes of our interview."

"That's fine with me."

Nick sat on the bed. "How's business, Mr. Wilson?"

"If you are referring to New Millennium Films, as I've already confided in you, it could be better."

"I believe you said something about *Smoking Out a Killer* being over budget?"

"That is correct."

"You told me that you'd spoken to Natalie about the matter and requested that she bring in a new unit manager."

Wilson shifted in the chair. "Did I? I don't remember."

"Perhaps I heard it from someone else. Is it true?"

"Yes."

"Am I correct in saying that the outcome of your talk with Natalie was that she turned down your request?"

"You are."

"So Tony Biciano remained as unit manager."

"He did."

"What Natalie wants Natalie gets?"

"New Millennium *is* her company."

"Who would run the company if she stepped aside?"

"Natalie would still be in command, by virtue of her controlling interest in the firm."

"Yes, but if she relinquished day-to-day running of the company?"

"That's for the board of directors to decide."

"I presume you would be a contender."

"Certainly."

"Do you happen to know who would gain control of Natalie's controlling interest in the company if she were to die?"

"You'd have to ask Simon Cane. He's Natalie's designated executor."

"How would you feel if control went to Tony Biciano?"

"If Natalie left her shares to Tony, how I might feel would be irrelevant."

"Except for the incident outside Natalie's hotel in Boston, were you aware that there had been other attempts made to kill her?"

"I was not. Where? When?"

"Natalie says they occurred in California at the time of the preproduction meetings for *Smoking Out a Killer.*"

"This is news to me."

"But you did attend the meetings?"

"As business affairs manager for the company I had to be present."

"My next question is of a more personal nature."

"You want to know about my relationship with Natalie."

"It's not a matter of my wanting to know. I *need* to know."

"It's no secret that Natalie and I were once lovers."

"Until Tony Biciano came along?"

"Actually, Natalie and I had ended our affair prior to then."

"You ended it on an amicable note, obviously. You stayed on at New Millennium Films."

"My remaining was in both our interests. She respects my business judgment."

"Except in the case of the unit manager on *Smoking Out a Killer*."

"She can respect my judgment without always accepting it."

"In your judgment, how would Tony do if he took over the company?"

"I don't believe that will happen."

"But if it did?"

"Tony would be a disaster."

"How about Richard Edwards?"

"Rich would be far more acceptable to me."

"Switching the subject now. What were you drinking last night?"

"I had a whiskey and soda before dinner, wine with the meal, and a brandy while we were waiting in the parlor for you to begin your talk."

"Did you talk with Natalie in the parlor?"

"No. We were to have a meeting in her office after your presentation."

"On what subject?"

"We were to discuss my concerns over the film's continuing budget problems. However, those concerns are now moot. I cannot imagine Natalie continuing production of the film."

"So from your standpoint, Harry's death was a good thing."

Wilson shot to his feet. "I find that remark extremely offensive, sir."

"You're right. That was badly phrased. I didn't mean it personally. I apologize. I meant to say that, in terms of budget problems, Harry's death has resolved them, because the production is probably going to be scrapped."

Wilson resumed his seat. "That does not make Harry's death less tragic."

"Tragic, certainly. It's also ironic in that the poisoned cognac was intended for Natalie."

"Apparently."

"Have you any idea who could have hated her enough to put cyanide in her drink?"

"I can name several people, none of whom was present last night."

"Where were you seated in the parlor?"

"My chair was directly in front of Harry's."

"At what time were you at the bar?"

"I had no occasion to be at the bar. The maid brought me the brandy. Speaking of a tragic event! Have you considered the likelihood that she was murdered because she'd seen something? Perhaps she observed the person who poisoned the cognac. Maybe she was involved somehow with whoever did this."

"I'm sure the police will look into that possibility."

"By the way, how was she killed? Was she also poisoned?"

"Her throat was cut."

Wilson grimaced. "How horrible. It happened when—during the night?"

"The murder appears to have occurred just before you and the others came into the dining room for breakfast."

"Now that I think about it, I wondered why she wasn't there to serve it."

"I'm sure these events have been a shock to you, Mr. Wilson, and I am sorry to have to subject you to questioning, but I'm sure you realize that someone in this house is the killer. And the one who was the killer's intended victim was Natalie Goodman."

"I trust steps are being taken to guard her."

"Tony Biciano is with her, and the police will be here as soon as the weather breaks."

Wilson turned to the window. "It can't be too soon!"

"I have one other request of you, Mr. Wilson. There's a notepad on the table beside you. Would you please print your name on it?"

Wilson looked at the pad quizzically. "May I ask why?"

"I assure you it's not because Professor Woolley and I are autograph collectors."

"Very droll, Mr. Chase," said Wilson as he printed his name.

Thirty-three

WHILE NICK WAITED for the next guest to arrive to be interviewed, he returned his attention to eating his breakfast.

Woolley was smoking a pipe at the window and assaying the weather.

"I believe the storm is letting up a little."

Nick nibbled cold bacon. "Remind me never to live on an island."

Woolley turned. "But you did. Manhattan is an island, you know."

"I think the first two interviews went very well, don't you?"

"Frankly, I thought your questions were all over the lot." Nick chuckled. "As in a movie lot?"

"The way you were bouncing between subjects you had my head spinning."

"The technique is what Muhammad Ali used to call the rope a dope. When I was in the police academy, it was called the keep 'em guessing and always off balance game. The theory is that if you stay on one line of questioning, the person you're interviewing will anticipate the next one and the one after that and—"

"I've gotten your point."

"What do you make of our first two visitors?"

"I don't care much for either of them."

"Neither do I, but is one of them a murderer?"

Three quick knocks drew Woolley to the door.

With Parker Slade at his side, Rich Edwards asked, "Are you ready for us?"

Woolley replied, "We're doing this one at a time."

"It's all right," said Nick, waving them into the room. "What's the show business term for two for the price of one?"

Rich answered, "A twofer."

"Suppose you take the chair over by the window, Rich, and Parker the one by the bureau. Would you fellas care for some coffee? I'm afraid it's on the tepid side."

Both declined and took their designated chairs.

Nick looked from one to the other. "I'm going to be right up front with you. I know about a certain videotape."

Edwards shrugged. "Apparently everyone in this house knows about it."

"What I don't know," said Nick, "is what you meant when you told Parker on the yacht not to worry, that you'd handle the problem with Natalie and, quote, it will be settled for good tonight, unquote."

Edwards clucked his tongue. "Professor Woolley, I am very disappointed. I would never have thought you would be a common eavesdropper."

"Eavesdropper, yes. But never common. There's a lesson in this for you, Mr. Edwards. Be careful what you say around writers. They are all eavesdroppers."

"What I meant by those words you inadvertently overheard—a much better way to put it, I think—is that it was my intention to discuss that tape with Natalie and tell her that whatever she decided to do about it would be fine with me. If she fired me, okay. If she didn't, great."

Nick asked, "Have you had the discussion?"

"We were going to meet after your cigar demonstration."

Nick glanced at Woolley. "Natalie had quite a busy night in store."

"What happened to Harry Hardin," Edwards continued, "has delayed us in doing so."

"But you still intend to meet."

"That's up to Natalie."

"Who do you think has been trying to kill her?"

"I have no idea."

Nick turned to Slade with a smile. "I understand that being in *Smoking Out a Killer* is a big opportunity for you. A breakthrough film."

Slade smiled nervously. "I certainly hope so."

"Are you concerned that because of the nature of the tape we've been talking about, you might lose out on that opportunity?"

Slade looked lovingly at Edwards. "I'm confident Rich will smooth everything out."

"Of course, with Natalie out of the way there would be no tape problem, right?"

Edwards said explosively, "Now just a damn minute. Are you accusing Parker of trying to kill Natalie to stay in the film? That is ridiculous!"

"I haven't accused anyone of anything."

Slade interjected, "Even if Natalie were out of the way, there's no guarantee that whoever took over from her would keep me in the picture."

"Unless the person who took over," Nick said, "was Richard Edwards."

"You are on the wrong track here, Nick," said Edwards. "Whether Parker continues in *Smoking Out a Killer* or doesn't, he will enjoy a brilliant future in movies."

"What about your future, Rich? If Natalie were dead, wouldn't your career benefit?"

"That's a hideous thing to say. Natalie has already named me producer of the next New Millennium film."

"If one of these attempts on Natalie's life had succeeded, who would have been put in charge of production on *Smoking Out a Killer?*"

"I suppose that would depend upon who took over the helm of New Millennium."

"What if that person were Tony Biciano?"

"Tony and I have a good professional relationship. I'm confident he would promote me to the job of producer on this film."

"There's no way to handle this next subject delicately, and frankly I'm not interested in digging around in people's dirty laundry, but when you're dealing with murder, it has to be gloves off time."

Edwards looked toward Slade. "Parker, why do I have a feeling that Nick is about to ask me if my relationship with Tony extends beyond the professional?"

Slade smirked. "Go ahead and ask him, Nick. I didn't just roll into town and fall off a turnip truck. Rich and I have no secrets. I know all about what went on between Rich and Tony. I also know it's over between them."

"Very well," Nick said with a shrug, "I'll move on. I presume the two of you have talked about what happened last night?"

Edwards answered, "How could we not?"

"Were either of you in a position in the parlor to observe the people at the bar?"

Slade replied, "We were at the bar ourselves—a couple of times, in fact, until Natalie announced it was being closed for your talk."

"Did either of you observe anyone lurking in Natalie's immediate proximity?"

Edwards leaned forward in his chair. "Such as someone slipping something into Natalie's snifter of cognac? Nick, if either of us had seen anything like that happen, don't you think that we certainly would have said something to you before now?"

"Did either of you notice the maid?"

Edwards sank back in the chair. "When I'm at a party, I pay no attention to maids. But a good-looking waiter or butler is quite another matter."

"There was a bartender."

Edwards smiled and rolled his eyes. "Bill Restivo!"

Nick returned to his cold breakfast. "I think that's all I need to know, guys. Thanks for your time and cooperation."

They rose to leave.

Nick slapped his forehead. "I almost forgot. I'd like each of you to print your name on the notepad by Rich's chair."

"I don't know about this," Edwards said lightheartedly as he picked up the pen. "Simon Cane would not approve of me putting my name on blank paper. But what the hell, I never pay attention to lawyers."

When they were gone, Woolley made a sour face. "What a cagey pair. A couple of cool cucumbers. Two peas in a pod."

Nick collected the two sheets of notepaper. "What? No allusion to fruits?"

"I told you I am not a homophobe," Woolley said, irritably. "I just don't like those two. It's obvious they rehearsed what they would say if you brought up the subject of their disgusting pornographic video."

"The performance came off very well."

"I'm surprised that you didn't interview them separately. I thought that was standard police procedure when dealing with two suspects who might be accomplices."

"It is indeed, but, as you said, they had time to rehearse what they would say. Why should I waste my time watching two performers doing the same act?"

"You've talked to four of the men who were in the dining room," said Woolley, sitting in the chair three of them had occupied. "That leaves Branson, Stevens, Biciano, Ivo Bogdanovich, Bill Restivo, and the cook."

"Even though Nora found Felicity, I believe we can dispense with the maxim of homicide investigation that the person who finds the body is probably the murderer."

As Nick headed for the door, Woolley picked up the notepad and pen.

"I won't be needing them, old friend," Nick said. "I already know which hand all the others use for writing."

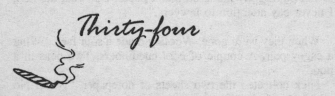

Thirty-four

IN THE FOLLOWING half hour Woolley observed Nick's questioning of Ivo Bogdanovich and Bill Restivo in their small bedroom. He questioned them about where they were in the parlor and what they'd seen. Several questions to Restivo dealt with what liquor each of the guests had been drinking after dinner. He asked about Natalie's bottle of cognac, inquiring how long it had been left standing unattended on the bar, and learned that it had been there, along with all the other liquor bottles, since Restivo had set up the bar shortly after their arrival on the island.

Nick asked about the handling of glasses after cocktails on Saturday.

"Those that had been used were collected and taken to the kitchen for washing later, along with the dishes and glassware from the dinner. There were plenty of glasses available, so there was no need to recycle the ones that had been used."

"How many brandy snifters were on the table?"

"I don't recall exactly how many. Probably three or four."

After dinner had any one of the guests partaken of Natalie's cognac?

Restivo had to think about it. "I don't think so."

Had he been surprised that no drinks were to be served during Nick's talk on cigars?

"Not at all," Restivo replied. "As soon as we landed Friday afternoon, Natalie asked to speak to me about her plans for Friday and Saturday night. As it turned out when I went to see her in her office, she was on the phone with an important call, so I wound up discussing the arrangements with Tony. He said he'd suggested to Natalie that the bar be closed during your talk to be sure that all the guests paid attention to you, and that Natalie thought it was a good idea."

Questioning of Ivo Bogdanovich, Woolley thought, was surprisingly brief and began with how long he'd been working for New Millennium Films.

Ivo answered, "Ever since Natalie started it."

"How did you land the job?"

"On the recommendation of Tony Biciano. I'd met him when I was working on a movie that Tony had a small part in."

"Was it Natalie's custom to hold meetings at her house near Santa Barbara?"

"I wouldn't say it was customary. She had a few meetings when we were shooting the picture before this one, *Affair in Venice*."

"It was written by—"

"Sheila Stevens. It was a bomb. Natalie blamed it on Sheila's script. But I thought that was a bum rap. Nothing went right on that film. That's why everyone at New Millennium has pinned their hopes on *Smoking Out a Killer* putting the company back into the black."

"One more question, Ivo. In your experience on movie sets, has anyone been hurt by a light falling over?"

"Not on any picture I've worked on, but I've heard of it happening."

"You told me the laundry room had been part of the old Nike missile base. How did you know that?"

"Tony told me about it on my first visit to the island. Natalie was having meetings here. Everyone was worried about the disappointing receipts from the *Affair in Venice*

turkey. That's when Natalie brought up acquiring the rights
to Mr. Woolley's book. She's very big on reading mystery
novels."

"I've noticed."

"*Affair in Venice* was a love story. Before that, New
Millennium had always made action films. Natalie said it
had been a mistake to switch the kind of pictures we'd been
making and she expected to get back on track and recoup
the losses of *Affair in Venice* by making *Smoking Out a
Killer*. That's why she brought in Cliff Branson to do a
treatment of the book instead of Sheila, and then to write
the screenplay."

"Do you know why she changed her mind, fired Cliff,
and went back to Sheila?"

"No, sir, but I do know Mr. Wilson hadn't been happy
about how things were going."

"You're referring to the business side of things, such as
Wilson's objections about Tony Biciano as unit manager?"

"Yes, sir."

Following the interviews with Ivo and Bill Restivo, Nick
sought out Sheila Stevens and found himself barred by Cliff
Branson.

"I don't think this is the right time," he objected. "And
who the hell empowered you to ask questions?"

Woolley asserted indignantly, "Nick has been authorized
by a lieutenant of the police of Portsmouth to make in-
quiries pending her arrival."

"Sheila will talk to the police and no one else."

"See here, sir!"

"It's quite all right, Professor," Nick said. "The questions
can wait."

As Branson closed the door to Sheila's room, Woolley
stared at it and grumbled, "What impertinence on that
man's part. How dare he treat you that way?"

Nick patted Woolley's back. "You would be impertinent,
too, if you were protecting the woman you were in love
with."

Woolley's eyes popped. "But Sheila's in love—was in love—with Harry Hardin."

"Who is now conveniently dead."

Woolley's jaw went momentarily slack. Tuggng at his beard, he muttered, "Is it possible that Branson—"

"Cliif Branson murdered Harry to get him out of the way? He might well have considered it, being a writer of money-making film thrillers, but the cyanide that killed Harry was placed in Natalie's glass."

When Nick sought to question Natalie, Tony Biciano expressed the same objection voiced by Branson, although more courteously, Woolley thought.

Again to Woolley's astonishment, Nick acquiesced.

Nick asked Tony, "How is she holding up in all this?"

Tony frowned. "Not very well. She's terribly distraught."

Woolley nodded. "Quite understandable."

Tony asked Nick, "How is your investigation going?"

"Very well, I believe."

As Nick and Woolley walked slowly along a hallway, Nick paused by one of the round windows they'd seen as *Murder Two* approached the island on Friday.

"The rain's stopped. The wind is down, too. If this trend continues, I expect we'll shortly be meeting Lieutenant Schneidau of the Portsmouth police. And very soon after that, my friend, you can take your tour of Smutty Nose Island, and I can get back to the business of selling cigars."

"Really? It seems to me this investigation has just begun."

"On the contrary. I'm pretty sure I've figured out the who."

Woolley gasped, "You have?"

Nick took out his cigar case and withdrew the last of the Coronas.

"Blast it, Nick," Woolley exclaimed, "I hate it when you're being coy."

Nick searched a pocket for a clipper.

"What I have to think about is the why," he said, trimming the cigar.

"Are you not going to tell me the who because you are afraid that at this late stage I won't be able to keep my mouth shut?"

Nick took his time lighting the cigar.

"That's not it at all, Professor," he said in a cloud of smoke. "You've been an invaluable ally. But now's the time for me to go over all the facts one more time. There's no hurry about it. No one's going to be leaving the island. I hope by the time Lieutenant Schneidau arrives that I'll be able to lay it all out for her. Then it will be a matter of arranging to get the confession."

PART IX

Smoking Out a Killer

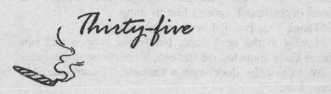

Thirty-five

WITH THE HELP of Ivo Bogdanovich and Bill Restivo, Nora completed laying out a buffet lunch of cold dishes in the dining room at noontime. Drapes had been opened to admit a weak sunlight struggling to get through thinning gray clouds. After a night of howling, buffeting winds, the house was quiet.

"I feel as if I've been watching a horror movie," said Ivo. "A big storm, a dead man in a chair in the parlor, and a maid with her throat cut in the basement."

Nora sobbed, "Poor sweet thing," and fled from the room.

"I also have a feeling," Ivo continued as he picked a fat shrimp from a bed of ice, "that it ain't anywhere near over."

"The trouble is," Bill said, following Ivo's lead and tasting the shrimp, "we're not in a movie theater, where we could get up and leave."

"Right," Ivo said, chewing, "and neither can the killer."

Bill stepped back from the buffet and looked at it admiringly for a moment. "It's so pretty it's a shame to disturb it, but I guess we'd better let the suspects know their lunch is ready."

"Nora said we're to take trays to Natalie and Tony."

"I'll take care of that," Bill said, helping himself to a last shrimp. "You can tell the others to come and get it."

When Ivo rapped once on the door of Nigel Wilson's room and announced that lunch was ready in the dining room, Wilson was again perusing financial records. The sound of the knock caused him to jump.

"Thank you, Ivo. I'll be there presently."

Moving to the next door, Ivo found it open and saw Simon Cane sprawled on the bed, a telephone in his hand.

Ivo tapped the door with a knuckle. "Excuse me, Mr. Cane. Lunch?"

The lawyer waved a hand that meant go away.

The announcement made through Sheila Stevens's door was answered by Cliff Branson. "Ivo, would you be so kind as to bring us something on a tray? Any old thing will do."

Ivo smiled a little at the thought of how Nora would react if she heard her food referred to as any old thing. "It will probably be a few minutes, Cliff."

"Whenever."

The knocking on Rich Edwards's door was answered by Parker Slade. "Who's there?"

"It's Ivo. Lunch is ready in the dining room."

After a long pause, Edwards said, "We'll be there in a few minutes."

Professor Woolley's and Nick's rooms were on the other side of the house. Woolley's door was wide open, and he was standing at the window, his back to Ivo.

"Excuse me, Mr. Woolley," Ivo said. "Lunch is ready. Nora's laid out quite a spread."

Woolley had been looking down at the boat landing. He turned slightly and smiled. "I'm not sure I'm all that hungry."

"No need to hurry. It's a cold buffet and there's plenty of it."

Woolley turned again to the window. "Perhaps later."

Nick opened his door after two knocks. "Ivo! What a coincidence. I was thinking about you. What can I do for you?"

"Lunch is ready in the dining room."

"Lunch already? What time is it?"

"A few minutes past twelve. Why were you thinking about me?"

"I've been thinking about everyone, actually. In your case I was recalling a conversation we had on the first day of shooting at my store. The one in which you told the joke about Natalie asking Simon Cane why everyone took an instant dislike to her."

"Cane said, 'Because it saves time.' What about it?"

"I also asked you why the whole picture wasn't shot in a studio. You said Natalie decided to go on location in Cambridge in order to take a trip down memory lane."

"And because she wanted to visit her house—this house."

"As I recall, you said something to the effect that everything Natalie does goes onto the budget of the film."

"That's right."

"Do you remember when she decided to shoot part of the picture in Cambridge?"

"I believe it was when we were having preproduction meetings."

"The ones that were held at her ranch?"

"Yes."

"Thanks, Ivo."

"Will you be having lunch?"

"Not right now."

"I could bring it to you on a tray."

"That's very kind, but if I want something, I'll go and get it myself."

Ivo looked toward the window. "The sky seems to be brightening. I suppose now that the storm is over and boats can go out again, the police will be showing up pretty soon."

"When they arrive, a Lieutenant Fran Schneidau, a woman, by the way, will ask for me. Please show her to my room."

Ivo winked. "Is that when you plan to tell her who the killer is?"

"I appreciate your confidence in me."

"I'm counting on you, Nick. I've got a bet with Bill

Restivo that you'll be the one who'll solve these murders."

With Ivo gone, Nick sat in the chair that had been occupied by those he'd questioned, but with the chair now
facing the window and providing a view of the calming
water. If the storm that was clearing had occurred twenty-
four hours earlier, he thought, lighting up a cigar, *Murder
Two* would have remained snugly and safely docked in
Portsmouth, no one would have boarded her at Rowes
Wharf in Boston, and this terrible weekend could not have
happened. Nick Chase would be contentedly serving customers of The Happy Smoking Ground.

Were it possible for him to order a revision in the script
that had brought him to Pirate's Cove, at what point might
a screenwriter such as Sheila Stevens or Cliff Branson place
a novel other than Roger Woolley's *Smoking Out a Killer*
in Natalie's hands? What if Natalie were not a fan of mysteries but had a penchant for romances? Histories? Biog-
raphy? Perhaps westerns?

Nobody made westerns anymore. In Nick's youth they
were called cowboy movies. What had happened to America, he wondered, to render cowboys pictures obsolete?

Even mysteries on screen had changed. Once upon a time
if someone was shot in the movies, the actor just dropped.
Now you had to see blood spurting out of the bullet hole.
The police had been the good guys, and if they were shown
to be inept, there had been a basically decent private eye
or some other amateur sleuth to solve the case—a suave
William Powell as sophisticated Nick Charles, never letting
a corpse stand in the way of him downing a martini, with
the charming and beautiful Myrna Loy as Nora matching
him drink for drink.

Movie murders had always been complicated, sometimes
so much so that it was hard to follow Charlie Chan's or
Bulldog Drummond's or the Saint's or Mr. Moto's explanation. But even in a bewildering story he'd usually spot
the villain simply by recognizing that a particular actor was
always the bad guy.

Somewhere, sometime, somehow all the rules of movies

had been thrown out. Good guys were no longer as good as they seemed. And neither were women.

Too bad, Nick thought. He held the cigar over an ashtray, gave it a gentle tap to let the long featherlight ash fall into it, and turned his mind from old and better movies to the murders that had been committed while a storm battered Pirate's Cove Island.

Thirty-six

A COAST GUARD launch eased dockside shortly after four o'clock in the afternoon. Wearing a floppy yellow rain hat and long yellow slicker, Lieutenant Fran Schneidau stepped ashore with two of her men, Sergeant Hy Turner and Officer Russ Bomberger, similarly outfitted. Nick and Woolley were there to greet them.

After introductions, Schneidau asked Nick, "Where are you holding the killer?"

He blinked. "Pardon me?"

"Mr. Woolley promised that when I got here you'd hand over the murderer."

"And I was right about that," said Woolley excitedly. "Nick does indeed know who it is. All that remains is to arrange to get a confession."

"Then why are we standing here on the dock?"

"Before I explain my thinking," Nick said as they headed toward the house, "I'd like you to see the bodies. Then, if you agree, I'll need your men to remove Harry Hardin so we can bring the suspects together in that room."

That done and with everyone assembled in the parlor, Nick said, "Please take the places you occupied last night when I was giving my talk."

They waited with expectant expressions as Nick began to speak.

"Please bear with me while I review the sequence of events which has brought all of us to this moment. To borrow a line from the New Testament, 'In the beginning was the word.'"

"Good lord, Nick," said Cliff Branson. "I hope you're not going to do what every film producer does when someone has to be hung out to dry. Blame a writer."

"In this instance," Nick said, "we start with the hundred thousand words of Woolley's novel *Smoking Out a Killer*. It was read by an old friend. Natalie Goodman thought it would make a good movie, and she obtained the rights to do so."

"And she paid a pretty price for them," said Nigel Wilson grumpily.

"A writer was chosen to do a treatment and develop the script," Nick continued, pacing the parlor. "The intent was to shoot the film in a studio. Preproduction meetings were then held at Natalie's ranch near Santa Barbara. All the principal figures of New Millennium Films attended. Hanging over the meetings like a dark cloud was the fact that the company's latest venture, *Affair in Venice*, was a financial disaster. Everyone believed that *Smoking Out a Killer* would redress that setback. Much of the optimism was based on Natalie having signed Harry Hardin, a proven box office winner, to star in the picture." He stopped pacing and made a slight bow to Simon Cane. "It was quite a deal for all the parties."

"If that's an aspersion—"

"It's a statement," Nick said with a shrug. "At preproduction meetings Natalie decreed that some of the scenes would be shot on location at my store in Cambridge. The schedule was arranged so that Natalie would be able to visit her house on this island. Why did she insist on this change of plan? At a dinner with me after the first day of shooting, she told me that she believed someone was trying to kill her. She cited three attempts—someone tried to run her car off a freeway, a bullet had been fired into her ranch house, and that very day she was nearly hit by a falling light. During our dinner, she presented to me a list of persons she believed had motives to kill her." He looked at Natalie. "Isn't that right?"

"As I recall," she said, "you were dubious."

"You then informed me that you had invited everyone on the list to spend the following weekend at Pirate's Cove. You wanted me to attend in the hope that I could find out which of those on your list was behind the four attempts on your life."

"Have you?"

"We'll see. I tried to persuade you to turn the matter over to the police. When I failed in that endeavor, I was left with no other choice but to agree to join all of you on *Murder Two* for the trip to Pirate's Cove. That evening a shot was fired at Natalie as we left the restaurant and another in front of her hotel." He paused and looked at them one after another, then continued. "To use a movie term, cut to Rowes Wharf, where we all boarded *Murder Two* on Saturday morning. On that enlightening voyage, I and Professor Woolley were able to confirm that each of you appeared to have not only a motive to kill Natalie, but the opportunity to have tried to do so in each of the attempts, either alone or with an accomplice."

He stood in front of Sheila Stevens.

"What was your motive?"

"This is your show, Nick. You tell me."

"You believed Natalie was going to fire you as the writer of *Smoking Out a Killer* and replace you with Cliff Edwards. You made it clear to me that this meant nothing to you financially. You'd get paid whether or not your script was used."

"There goes my motive."

"However, you would be deprived of screen credit, and that embarrassment—humiliation, even—would be on top of the knowledge in the film industry that your previous film, *Affair in Venice,* had been a flop. Your reputation was in the balance. But if Natalie were dead, *Smoking Out a Killer* would probably be abandoned, and you would walk away with both your money and your reputation."

"All that is true," Sheila retorted. "But I didn't try to kill Natalie."

Nick approached Simon Cane. "As Natalie's executor, you stood to gain the power of that position and a very considerable executor's fee. You would also no longer have a conflict of interest in representing Natalie and Harry Hardin."

Cane smiled smugly. "Poppycock."

"Nigel Wilson," Nick said, turning to him, "dearly desires to be a movie producer."

"Is ambition a crime?"

"It is if it leads to murder. Natalie's death would clear the way for you to influence the members of the board so that you could take over control of New Millennium Films."

Cliff Branson raised a hand. "What's my motive, Nick?"

"You were removed from *Smoking Out a Killer*. Revenge has always been a powerful motive for murder.

"But I was about to be reinstated."

"Yes, and because of that Natalie told me to disregard you as a suspect. However, simply because she no longer regarded you as a threat to her life does not mean that you hadn't tried to kill her. Nor that you no longer nurtured animosity toward Natalie for having fired you in the first place. Therefore, in my book, you were still quite a viable suspect."

"Thank you. I'd hate to be left out."

Nick said, "And what of Richard Edwards?"

"You really should try your hand at fishing, Nick," he replied. "You're excellent at casting out a net."

"In addition to being in a position to profit professionally by the death of Natalie," Nick went on, "you suddenly found yourself in the awkward position of possibly being under Natalie's thumb because of a certain videotape that had come into her possession. Your friend and protégé, Parker Slade, found himself in the same boat with you. He was, perhaps, in even more jeopardy, because, despite Hollywood's reputation for being very liberal-minded about sex, there is still a profound fear that the moviegoing public might not pay to see the odd man out. I cite the cases of the late Rock Hudson and Sal Mineo. One managed to keep his proclivity for boys a secret from the public and prospered. The other came out of the closet and, well, you all know Mineo's sad story of being shut out of the business because he was openly gay."

"It so happens," objected Rich Edwards, "that Sal Mineo wasn't able to make the difficult transition from teenage idol to leading man."

"I'm aware of the official Hollywood version," Nick replied. "However, I am a little surprised that a gay man would buy into it and repeat it."

"Haven't you wandered off your point?"

"Yes, I have. Now, to use another movie term, we flash forward to Saturday night and the death of Harry Hardin by a glass of poisoned cognac. I must admit that I was caught off guard. I had to ask myself why was it necessary to introduce cyanide into Natalie's glass? Bill Restivo says that the bottle had been standing on the bar for hours. In that case, why not put the cyanide in the bottle?"

"It seems perfectly clear to me," interjected Cliff Branson, "that the killer didn't want to run the risk of someone else pouring a glass of the cognac before Natalie did."

"My conclusion exactly," Nick said. "But that brings us back to how Natalie's glass was poisoned. It had to have been done under the nose of Bill Restivo."

Nigel Wilson exclaimed, "He could have done it."

"Why should Bill want to poison the woman he was hoping would be so impressed with him that she would give him a role in *Smoking Out a Killer*? That was Bill's only reason for accepting Tony Biciano's offer of the job of bartender for this weekend."

"Okay, Bill didn't do it. So who the hell did?"

"To answer that, we must review what happened last night as I was preparing to give my little talk on cigars. Before I began, you all came into this room for after-dinner drinks. All of you had the opportunity to go to the bar."

Woolley interjected, "Any of you might have waited until Bill Restivo's attention was directed to pouring drinks and put the cyanide into a cognac glass."

Restivo shook his head violently. "No. I never pour a drink without examining the glass. The poison had to be put in after the cognac was poured."

Nick asked, "Did you pour it for Natalie?"

Restivo thought a moment. "No, she poured it herself."

"That's correct," Natalie said. "So the cyanide must have been put into the snifter when I set it down. I went to speak to you, remember?"

"Yes, I do. You then went back to the bar, told everyone to take seats, and announced that the bar was closed."

"Yes. I wanted everyone to pay attention to your talk."

"I appreciate that, Natalie, but why did you insist that Bill also take a seat?"

"For the same reason."

"Why did it matter to you that Bill pay attention to my talk?"

"I'd decided to take Tony's advice and give the young man a part in the film. I wanted everyone involved in the picture to benefit from your talk, from your expertise."

"Where was Felicity Dane at the time?"

"I really don't recall."

"Do you recall telling her that she was not to serve any food?"

"I do remember that."

"During my talk you remained at the bar?"

"I believe so. I found your lecture fascinating."

"Thank you," said Nick.

He moved to Tony Biciano. "We come now to the moment when I was passing out cigars and clippers and Tony bumped Harry's arm, causing him to spill a drink. At that point, Natalie gave Harry her cognac, and we all saw what happened."

Tony exclaimed, "Who could forget it? Harry got poison that was meant for Natalie."

"Or so it seemed."

"What the devil do you mean by that?" demanded Tony.

Nick stepped away from him and stood before Rich Edwards. "What impact will Harry's death have on *Smoking Out a Killer?*"

"Production will be stopped until we find someone to replace him."

"An actor who'll cost a lot less?"

Edwards laughed nervously. "If you are proposing that Harry was killed to save money, you know nothing about the movie business. Simon Cane will tell you that Harry always got his salary up front."

Cane said, "That's right."

Nick moved to Nigel Wilson.

"As the man overseeing the budget of *Smoking Out a Killer*," he asked, "how did you feel about that arrangement?"

"I didn't like it. I advised against signing Harry Hardin for that very reason."

"Because I know nothing about the movie business, as Tony points out," Nick continued with Wilson, "please educate me about what happens when the star of a movie is unable to complete a film."

"There's usually litigation."

Nick turned to Simon Cane. "Can you sue a dead man?"

"You can sue his estate."

"That would be a pretty awkward case for you, I should think. You'd represent both New Millennium Films, the complainant, and Harry's estate as the defendant."

"If you had allowed me to finish," Cane said, "I would have said that the matter would in all likelihood be covered by the insuring entity that issued the completion policy."

Nick smiled and turned toward Clifford Branson. "How did that little poem go that you recited for Woolley and me on the yacht?"

Branson looked puzzled. "Poem?"

Nick looked toward Woolley. "Do you happen to recall it, Professor?"

"I do indeed. It's from 'Etiquette' by W. S. Gilbert:

*And down in fathoms many went the captain and
 the crew;
Down went the owners—greedy men whom hope
 of gain allured:
Oh, dry the starting tear, for they were heavily
 insured."*

"For they were heavily insured," said Nick, returning to
Nigel Wilson. "In the event of the death of Harry Hardin
how much money will New Millennium Films be entitled
to claim under Harry's completion policy?"

"Why, the full amount of his salary. I don't recall the
exact sum. The insurance will pay for other expenses incurred, as well."

"Would that payout be enough to put New Millennium
back into the black on your ledger sheets, Mr. Wilson?"

He shifted nervously. "I suppose so."

"A man like you doesn't suppose, Mr. Wilson. He knows
down to the penny. But never mind. You've answered my
question sufficiently to explain why Harry was murdered."

Sheila Stevens jumped up and shrieked, "Harry was *murdered?*"

Nick replied, "Oh, yes. Harry's death was not an accident."

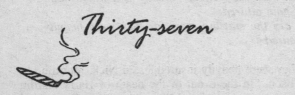

Thirty-seven

"EVERYTHING IN THIS amazing drama was scripted months ago," Nick continued quietly. He lifted both arms as if he were trying to embrace everyone in the room. "Each of you played your role magnificently. How did the Bard of Avon, good old Will Shakespeare put it? 'They have their exits and their entrances.' "

Rich Edwards clapped. "Bravo, Nick. Where did you learn that?"

"In Miss Kelly's English class. We all had to memorize that speech."

"May we hear more?"

"As to your assigned roles," Nick continued, "You all deserve Oscars in the supporting actor category."

Silence fell again, and Woolley's gaze searched wondering, worried faces.

"But the top award," said Nick, "has to be presented to an astonishing auteur—the writer, producer, director, and leading lady."

He dipped a hand in a pocket and drew out a cigar.

"I regret I have no golden statuette to give you, Natalie," he said, going toward the bar, "so I guess this will have to do."

Natalie threw back her head and laughed loudly.

"You devised a magnificent plan," Nick said, returning

the cigar to the pocket. "But as a former Sixties revolutionary, why wouldn't you?"

Natalie glared at him. "What plan was that?"

"My son Kevin, a very cynical newspaperman, believed that I was being suckered into a publicity stunt. It took me quite a while to recognize that I was being used in a much grander scheme. The purpose was to save New Millennium Films by murdering Harry Hardin and collecting on his completion insurance."

He left Natalie and went to the spot where he'd lectured on cigars.

"I'd not known of such a thing as completion insurance until I heard the term a couple of times in the past two days. The plan was to make it appear that Harry died by drinking poisoned cognac that was intended for Natalie. In order for this to work it had to be established that someone had been trying to kill her. That's where I came in. Why me? The dubious distinction came to me because Natalie had read the novel Professor Woolley loosely based on me. In order to get me involved, she needed to acquire the film rights to Woolley's book. Enough money and a past with Woolley assured that she would. But now the plan that was developing depended on what every movie needs to succeed—a cast and crew. Movies are a collaborative effort, and so must be the murder of Harry Hardin."

Nick approached Simon Cane. "You arranged the deal that brought Harry onto the film."

Turning to Nigel Wilson, he said, "You handled obtaining the completion insurance."

Looking round the room, he continued, "Everyone else was to play his or her part by pretending for my benefit. That was why Natalie arranged to bring you all here on her yacht. But first she had to be sure I would be on board."

Woolley looked at Natalie and saw the same defiant expression that he had seen during a protest against Nixon decades ago at the Copley Plaza Hotel.

"Hence Natalie's invitation to me to have dinner with her at Farley's," Nick went on. "That's what tweaked my interest. As I said to Woolley, when a woman like Natalie

Goodman asks me to dinner, she's got more on her mind than good food and conversation. Of course, she expected me to be suspicious. The bait on her hook was a shot outside Farley's and another outside her hotel."

He went to Sheila Stevens. "I suspected you could have done that."

"Impossible. Harry told you I was making love to him."

"Harry could have lied."

"Why would he?"

"Because he loved you."

He moved toward Tony Biciano.

"But I believe now that it was you who fired the shot outside the Copley Plaza."

Tony blared, "I was asleep in Natalie's suite."

"So Natalie said. You probably also put the bullet through the window of Natalie's house at Santa Barbara."

Tony sneered. "Did I also try to run her car off the freeway?"

"That never happened."

"And the light that fell?"

"You gave it a shove."

"Can you prove any of this?"

"Certainly not. That was the beauty of Natalie's script," Nick said, walking to the bookcases that bracketed Natalie's portrait.

He ran a fingertip along the spines of the books.

"Her obviously voracious reading of detective novels," he said, "has made her a master of the art of placing red herrings, deflection, diversion of attention, and overall deception. She used those skills to concoct a bewildering variety of motives to kill her. You learned your lines well. But she was also careful to create a scenario in which there would be no actual evidence for me to find."

He turned from the books and looked across the parlor to Natalie behind the bar.

"That's why she needed to make certain that everyone in this room was looking at me when she put the cyanide into her glass. Then it was a matter of waiting for Tony to cause Harry to spill his drink."

He stood before Tony again.

"I presume the scene was rehearsed many times so that when the time came for you to play it for real, it would be done in one take."

"You missed your calling, Nick. You should be a screenwriter. But as I said, you can't prove any of this."

"That's true. However, I can prove that you murdered someone who was not anticipated in Natalie's original plan, namely Felicity Dane."

"Now, why would I do that?"

"For the same reason you went along with Natalie's scheme to murder Harry. You had no choice, except to walk away from Natalie's plan. Of course, that would have meant no marriage and no future in the movie business. As to the specific reason for your murder of Felicity, I can only speculate that Felicity saw Natalie poison the cognac. Alas, Felicity made the mistake of trying to blackmail Natalie. My guess—and it is a guess—is that Felicity made her demands when she brought you and Natalie breakfast. This conjecture is based on Felicity having been seen as she was taking a tray to Natalie's suite."

Nick turned to Simon Cane.

"You blundered there, Counselor. You shouldn't have told me you saw Felicity in the corridor. She was killed immediately after you saw her. That it happened in the laundry room, I surmise, is because that's where Natalie instructed her to wait for Tony to arrange the payoff."

"These are guesses, all right," Tony exclaimed. "Just as you can't prove that I fired any shot at Natalie or pushed over the light, you have no proof that I killed the maid."

"But I do."

Nick turned to Schneidau.

"The girl's throat was cut from behind, right to left," she explained.

"It's the unmistakable indication," said Nick, drawing his left hand across his neck from right to left, "that the wound was made by a left-handed person. Correct, Lieutenant?"

"The coroner will confirm it when he does the autopsy."

"And you, Tony," Nick said, leaning close to him and

tapping a finger on Tony's left wrist, "are the only south-paw on this island."

Tony squirmed. Nick came up straight.

"Lieutenant Schneidau," he continued, "is that reasonable cause to make an arrest?"

"It is," she declared, "and I do."

Sergeant Turner and Officer Bomberger bracketed Tony.

"Whether you're enough of a fool to take the fall for everyone in Natalie's conspiracy to kill Harry Hardin is entirely up to you, Tony," Nick said. "For what it's worth to you, I have never regarded you as a fool. Also for what it's worth, my advice is that when you look for an attorney, don't even think about retaining Simon Cane. That was Harry Hardin's mistake."

He withdrew the cigar from his pocket, trimmed it, lighted it, and took a few puffs.

"As to the rest of you, with the exception of Ivo Bog-danovich, Bill Restivo, Nora, and Sheila Stevens, whom I'm pretty sure had nothing to do with this sorry scenario, how the courts of New Hampshire treat you will be a matter of how cooperative you are. How much you assist in the investigation will go a long way in determining how much time you spend in prison."

Thirty-eight

DUSK WAS RAPIDLY giving way to night as Nick and Woolley sat by the parlor window. Nick was smoking a cigar. Woolley had a pipe going.

They watched six officers of the Portsmouth Police Department debark from two boats and march up the walkway to the house.

"Who could have imagined when we boarded *Murder Two* on Friday morning," Woolley said, "that we were entering the Calais coach of the Orient Express?"

Nick removed the cigar from his mouth. "I'm afraid I don't follow you."

"In *Murder on the Orient Express*, they *all* did it."

"Ah, yes, of course," said Nick, chuckling. "But in this case, not all. Sheila Stevens was not a part of it. Neither, I think, was Cliff Branson involved, except as a pawn. I could be wrong. Schneidau will have to sort that out."

Woolley nodded. "She's got a long night ahead of her."

The sound of the police officers entering the house reached the parlor.

Woolley puffed his pipe. "What was your first clue?"

"I found it odd when we were aboard *Murder Two* that no one was talking about the shots that had been fired at Natalie the previous night."

"I suppose that was because they'd known in advance that it was planned."

"Possibly. But I think Natalie improvised it to convince me that she'd told me the truth about the attempts on her life. Because the shot was not in the script, everyone was reluctant to talk about it."

"You may be right."

"But they were very good at following the rest of Natalie's script. They skillfully fed us plausible motives for killing Natalie."

"What a cool customer she was in staging that macabre game of how would you kill me."

"That game at dinner Friday evening had two purposes. The first was to further reinforce the story she'd told me about her belief that someone was trying to kill her. I believe it was also a signal to her coconspirators that she was going ahead with her plan to kill Harry Hardin. But she went too far with the note that I was told had been slipped under her door stating that the time for games was over. It made no sense. Why would someone who'd made four attempts to kill her suddenly issue a warning?"

"I see your point."

"The note was meant to keep me interested, but it was overkill. In light of the fact that all the guests were convinced that I'd been brought to the island to discover who was trying to kill Natalie, only a fool would have left a note that might be traceable."

"I thought that was why you had each of the suspects print his name on that notepad. I had no idea you were looking for left-handers."

Nick smiled. "Neither did any of them, or one of them would have tried to mislead me by using his right hand. None did. I knew then that Tony Biciano was the only southpaw on the island. That took care of who'd killed Felicity. What I didn't know was why Harry Hardin had been murdered."

"What put you onto the insurance scheme?"

"Nigel Wilson had been feeding me information about New Millennium Films being in financial trouble. He did so, of course, to make me think that someone was trying to kill Natalie to keep from being caught playing games with the budget." He paused to smoke. "There was just too much stuff being shoveled my way. Wilson feeding me information about the company being in financial difficulty was intended to validate a possible motive for killing Natalie. That left me Tony Biciano as the possible culprit, because he'd taken over as unit manager."

"Devilishly clever," said Woolley through a puff of pipe smoke. "Each was pointing the finger at another."

"I expect that we'll learn as Schneidau questions Tony," Nick said, "that the reason the original unit manager, Cindy Raphael, was dismissed was so that she wouldn't discover that while the books showed the film to be running way over budget, hardly any money was being spent. I believe the police will discover when they examine the New Millennium books that the only funds that were expended were to acquire rights to your novel, the costs of that one day of shooting at my store, a few other minor items, and Harry Hardin's salary. I think they will find that the amount paid in the fulfillment of the completion insurance policy would not only cover money that had been paid to Harry Hardin, actual expenses incurred, and all the phony ones, but also provide enough to keep New Millennium Films from going bankrupt.

"In order for this plan to work, Natalie had to find a way to get Harry Hardin to Pirate's Cove. That problem was resolved by shooting a few scenes at my store."

"With Harry in Cambridge," said Woolley, "it was easier to lure him to Pirate's Cove."

"The bait was the story that Natalie was planning to fire Sheila Stevens. Natalie counted on Harry taking his screen persona to heart by playing the role of hero to the rescue in real life."

"What a dastardly plot!"

"Having planted the story about attempts on her life in my head, Natalie expected that in a police investigation into Harry's death I'd lend credence to Harry having been killed because he got Natalie's poisoned cognac accidentally.

While she knew that the police would conduct an investigation into who was trying to kill her, she was confident that despite a plethora of suspects the police wouldn't be able to prove anything. I certainly came up with nothing to prove that any of Natalie's guests for this weekend ever tried to harm her. All I had was motives. You can't put anyone in jail for simply wanting to kill someone. It was a good plan that might have worked."

"Then Felicity threatened to spoil everything," Woolley asserted, "and the girl had to be eliminated."

Nick tapped ash into an ashtray. "If they had paid Felicity off, they could have bought time and disposed of her later, after everyone had left Pirate's Cove."

Ivo Bogdanovich entered the parlor.

"Excuse me, guys, but Nora's got dinner ready in the kitchen. We can't use the dining room, because that's where the police are grilling Tony. I could bring you something here."

Nick rose. "You've done enough waiting on us, Ivo. The kitchen will be just fine."

As he passed the open door of the dining room, Schneidau stepped into the corridor, all smiles. "Tony is singing like a canary."

"I figured he would. He's a smart guy."

"You were right, Nick. The whole thing was a plot to bilk an insurance company. I'll haul the whole bunch out of here and into Portsmouth in a couple of hours."

"If you wish, I can write a report on what happened here from my point of view. It may fill in some blanks."

"That would be great."

She turned to go but paused and looked back.

"I presume you'll need transportation off the island."

"It would be a mighty long swim."

"I'll be happy to arrange it, but it won't be till tomorrow morning."

"Would it be possible," said Woolley, "for you to contact a man named Bob Gibson and ask if he can come out and pick us up?"

"As a person who enjoys fishing, I know Mr. Gibson very well."

"Wonderful! On the way to the mainland I'd like to visit one of the other islands."

"Smutty Nose?"

Woolley's eyes widened. "Have you been there?"

"I know it very well. You can't be this close to Smutty Nose and not visit the scene of the most notorious crime ever committed in these parts. Until now."

"Oh, my dear, what's the murder of a movie star by cyanide poisoning in an insurance scheme compared to two murders that were committed with an axe?"

Thirty-nine

As *CLARA BELLA* rounded the northeast point of Pirate's Cove at eleven o'clock Monday morning in brilliant sunshine, Bob Gibson thought back to the fishing expedition of Saturday and felt justified in having decided that he had never seen a queerer bunch of people. But it had never crossed his mind that they were a gang of murderers.

Yet that's what he'd heard in Portsmouth. Two people dead, one of them the movie star whose autograph he'd gotten and the other a maid. Some kind of craziness about collecting on an insurance policy. The person behind it, he'd been told, was Mrs. Goodman. This had come as a real shocker. He'd never liked her much—her husband was much nicer—but he never took her to be capable of killing anyone.

The big house came into view, and he wondered what would happen to it. To the best of his knowledge, the Goodmans had no children. The place, he assumed, would go on the real estate market. No doubt some rich person would buy it. Though why anyone would want to own a house where a couple of murders had been committed was beyond him.

Looking ahead to the dock, he saw four men and Nora Swanson waiting.

Nora, he hoped, would give him the whole story on what had happened on the island.

Three of the men had been out fishing with him on Saturday. Who the burly-looking, gray-haired man was he had no idea, except that he had the look of a cop. He knew every member of the Portsmouth force, so if that's what he was, he definitely was not a local lawman.

When *Clara Bella* gently kissed the dock, the Professor waved his arms and shouted, "Ahoy there, Bob. Much better weather today, eh?"

A few minutes later, they were heading toward Smutty Nose and the Professor was telling everyone the story of the murders that had happened there.

Louis Wagner rowing twelve miles from Portsmouth to the island. His plan to steal some money. The bad luck of one of the three women in the house waking up. Wagner's panic. Killing the woman with an axe. The other women screaming. Killing one of them and the other getting away. Rowing back to the mainland. Running off to Boston, only to be caught. Brought back to Portsmouth by the police. An angry mob with minds set on lynching him. A trial. Found guilty. Sentenced to be hanged. An escape, short-lived. The governor refusing to save him from hanging and telling Wagner that he looked like a man who had tried to murder his way out of trouble.

Finished recounting the tale, Woolley sat next to Nick at the stern of the boat and took out a pipe. "It's ironic isn't it?"

"What's ironic?"

"How history seems to have repeated itself. Natalie Goodman thought she could save her film company by murdering her way out of its financial difficulties. Yet in a perverse way, you have to admire her for the genius and originality of her plot."

"I'm not sure I can agree with you," Nick said.

"Really? Why not?"

"Last night, when I was having trouble getting to sleep," Nick said, "I went back to reading that book I borrowed from Natalie's library—*The Mirror Crack'd from Side to Side*."

"What of it?"

"A woman is murdered with a poisoned drink."

"Agatha Christie often despatched victims with poison. She'd made a study of poisons and liked to show off."

"The poisoned drink in this instance was given to the woman after she spilled her own."

Woolley shook his head. "I told you Christie grabbed all the best plots! But do you think Natalie got the idea from that book?"

Nick took out a cigar but decided there was too much wind to light it.

"If she did steal the idea, she'll never admit it," he said, putting the cigar into a pocket. "She's much too proud a woman."

Woolley puffed smoke. "And arrogant."

"That too."

"A remarkable woman, though."

"Very."

AN ARCHEOLOGIST DIGS UP MURDER IN THE ALAN GRAHAM MYSTERIES BY

MALCOLM SHUMAN

THE MERIWETHER MURDER
79424-1/$5.99 US/$7.99 Can

BURIAL GROUND
79423-3/$5.50 US/$7.50 Can

ASSASSIN'S BLOOD
80485-9/$5.99 US/$7.99 Can

And Coming Soon
PAST DYING
80486-7/$5.99 US/$7.99 Can

Available wherever books are sold or please call 1-800-331-3761 to order.   MSH 0200

Mysteries with a touch
of the mystical
by

JAMES D. DOSS

THE SHAMAN LAUGHS
72690-4/$5.99 US/$7.99 Can

THE SHAMAN SINGS
72496-0/$5.99 US/$7.99 Can

THE SHAMAN'S BONES
79029-7/$5.99 US/$7.99 Can

THE SHAMAN'S GAME
79030-0/$5.99 US/$7.99 Can

and in hardcover
THE NIGHT VISITOR
97721-4/$23.00 US/$34.00 Can

Available wherever books are sold or please call 1-800-331-3761
to order.   DOS 0300

The Boldest New Voice in Detective Fiction
DENNIS LEHANE

SACRED
72629-7/$6.99 US/$8.99 Can

Two private investigators, Patrick Kenzie and Angela Gennaro are caught in the middle between a dangerous cult that manipulates the needy and the mysterious disappearances of a grief-stricken woman and the detective hired to find her.

DARKNESS, TAKE MY HAND
72628-8/$6.99 US/$9.99 Can

"Haunting...heart-poundingly suspenseful."
People

A DRINK BEFORE THE WAR
72623-8/$6.99 US/$9.99 Can

"Move over Spenser...Score this one a smashing success"
Boston Globe

GONE, BABY, GONE
73035-9/$6.99 US/$8.99 Can

PRAYERS FOR RAIN
73036-7/$6.99 US/$9.99 Can

"The well-oiled plot mechanics, edge-of-the-knife dialogue and explosive bursts of violence are polished and primed in this hard-boiled shocker . . . fast-moving narrative." —*The New York Times Book Review*

Available wherever books are sold or please call 1-800-331-3761 to order.
DL 0300

Nationally Bestselling Author
of the Peter Decker and Rina Lazarus Novels

Faye Kellerman

"Faye Kellerman is a master of mystery."
Cleveland Plain Dealer

SACRED AND PROFANE
73267-X/$6.99 US/$9.99 Can

JUSTICE
72498-7/$6.99 US/$8.99 Can

SANCTUARY
72497-9/$6.99 US/$9.99 Can

PRAYERS FOR THE DEAD
72624-6/$6.99 US/$8.99 Can

SERPENT'S TOOTH
72625-4/$6.99 US/$9.99 Can

MOON MUSIC
72626-2/$7.50 US/$9.99 Can

THE RITUAL BATH
73266-1/$6.99 US/$8.99 Can

AND COMING SOON
JUPITER'S BONES
73082-0/$7.50 US/$9.99 Can

Available wherever books are sold or please call 1-800-331-3761
to order.   FK 0200

Alaska Mysteries by Award-winning Author

SUE HENRY

MURDER ON THE IDITAROD TRAIL
71758-1/$ 6.50 US/ $8.99 Can
"Dazzling...An adrenaline pumping debut"
The New York Times Book Review

TERMINATION DUST
72406-5/ $5.99 US/ $7.99 Can

SLEEPING LADY
72407-3/ $5.99 US/ $7.99 Can

DEATH TAKES PASSAGE
78863-2/ $6.99 US/ $8.99 Can

DEADFALL
79891-3/ $6.50 US/ $8.50 Can

MURDER ON THE YUKON QUEST
78864-0/ $6.50 US/ $8.99 Can

Jessie Arnold and her team of dogs are competing in the toughest dog sled race in the world—with an unknown killer on their trail.

Available wherever books are sold or please call 1-800-331-3761 to order.   SHE 0200

Edgar Award-winning author

EDNA BUCHANAN

"Buchanan again proves that she is the mistress of Miami crime...
deftly delivers on suspense and emotion."
—PUBLISHERS WEEKLY

CONTENTS UNDER PRESSURE
72260-7/$6.99 US/$8.99 Can

MIAMI, IT'S MURDER
72261-5/$6.99 US/$8.99 Can

PULSE
72833-8/$6.99 US/$8.99 Can

——— And in hardcover ———

GARDEN OF EVIL
A BRITT MONTERO NOVEL
97654-4/$24.00 US/$35.00 Can

Available wherever books are sold or please call 1-800-331-3761
to order.
EB 0200